Jack London's

Tales of Hawaii

Introduction by Miriam Rappolt

Press Pacifica   **Hawaii**

LIBRARY OF CONGRESS CATALOGING IN PUBLICATION

London, Jack, 1876-1916
  Jack London's Tales of Hawaii.

  Contents: Koolau, the leper — House of pride — Chun
Ah Chun — [etc.]
    I. Title.   II. Title: Tales of Hawaii.
PS3523.46A6   1982.   813'.52   81-23492
ISBN 0-916630-25-0   AACR2

Cover design, Maile Yawata.

Printed by Delta Lithograph, Van Nuys, CA 91411.

Available from: Press Pacifica, P.O. Box 1227, Kailua, Hawaii 96734.

THE TALES

Introduction

At least a dozen editions of Jack London's collections of short stories are in print today. But many of his readers do not even realize that he wrote many tales while visiting Hawaii, which add an entirely new dimension to his portfolio of outstanding works in print. Have readers summarily decided that the balmy islands of paradise are a feeble environment for the vigorous adventures of London's heroes fighting the hostile forces of Nature and Man? To stereotype a teller of tales of London's vigor and excellence shows lack of appreciation for his qualities of irony and social awareness, as well as for his appreciation of the delicate balance in the human comedy.

At the height of his popularity as a chronicler of northern climes, London commissioned the yacht *Snark*, installed a crew and his second wife aboard and sailed from San Francisco to Honolulu; he had tired of writing tales of the frozen North, and longed for some new adventure in a warmer climate to provide inspiration for his fertile pen. His intent was to explore the South Pacific, much as RLS (Robert Louis Stevenson) had done more than twenty years before. The vessel leaked badly, and the navigator confessed after they were well out to sea that he had never really navigated a boat; London was forced to sit down with books and sextant and teach himself the rudiments of this skill. After five trying weeks, the *Snark* limped into Honolulu harbor, to be left for repairs while the Londons installed themselves in a bungalow off Seaside Lane in Waikiki.

They were immediately swept up by the mainstream of Honolulu society. Jack and Charmian London drove around Oahu by carriage, stopping at the Hobron place in Pearl City one day, and taking lessons in riding surfboards from the *kanakas* at Waikiki Beach the next. They spent time with friends on Tantalus, and attended a reception for visiting congressmen given by Prince Jonah Kuhio Kalanianaole, Hawaii's delegate to Washington. There they also met the deposed Queen Liliuokalani. When he and his wife were not hiking up a slope like Diamondhead, the Londons were dining with Lorrin Thurston, publisher of the Honolulu Advertiser. Indeed, the circumstances of his stay, the folk with whom he rubbed elbows, would lead most readers to expect to find their fictional counterparts racing through his plots, creating adventure and intrigue.

Yet it is not these people, much as they interested London, who served as the principal inspiration for London's main characters. He was equally fascinated, for instance, with the plight of the leper in the islands, and spent several days at Kalauapapa on Molokai visiting the colony with his wife. The dilemma of the lepers weaves a strong thread through the plots of three of his Hawaii stories: "Good-Bye Jack," "Koolau the Leper," and "The Sheriff of Kona." In each story leprosy plays a different role, thus allowing the reader to view the impact of the disease from differing perspectives. The Jack of "Good-Bye, Jack," is a member of the upper strata of society, sympathetic to the lepers' plight in a detached sort of way—that is, until he discovers that he, Jack, has been directly exposed to the disease. "Koolau," on the other hand, presents the case from the point of view of the victim; London allows this Hawaiian man to live out his remaining years in exile in the mountains in Kauai, rather than on Molokai. He grants him power and dignity while he hides in the woods with his wife and child, eluding his *haole* pursuers. To complete the trilogy, "The Sheriff of Kona" has as its leading character a caucasian lawman, whose duty it is to seek out and isolate lepers hiding on the Big Island of Hawaii. He suffers the immediate conflicts of one who must perform such a distasteful task, but the story gains tragic power when it is revealed that he also has contracted the disease. Because he is a good and sympathetic *haole*, reluctantly performing his duty, his fate seems a greater tragedy. These three stories demonstrate London's sympathy for the leper as well as for those left behind; what is truly amazing is that he should paint such insightful portrayals after only a few months' visit.

When they were offered for sale, the stories sent wave after wave of indignation through the well-to-do community which had shown London such *aloha*. His duplicity, they averred, was shocking. These readers were outraged at what they felt was the stories' focus on leprosy and other negative aspects of life in the islands. So it is not suprising that the stories were not displayed on the shelves of the homes he had visited, and if Honolulu bookshops did stock the anthology, it was likely to be hidden away at the back out of sight.

London's reaction to angry letters in Honolulu's newspaper was to insist that he was being misread. To the accusation that he was a racist, London reminds his readers (through his letters to Lorrin Thurston) that the stories are fiction, first and last; that as often as the haoles are depicted as the strong, evil overlords, they are the weaker characters, as in "Good-Bye, Jack." He also depicts them as the protagonists, holding out against injustice, as the sheriff reacts in "The Sheriff of Kona." They are even, as in the story "Chun Ah Chun," presented as the most desirable element whom Chun wants his children to marry, London sets it up to make the caucasians, not the Chinese appear slightly foolish (in a refined way) when they accept Chun's money. Yet despite his friend Thurston's explanations, it appeared that the caucasian community had already closed ranks against the author.

London could not have been totally surprised by this reaction to his stories, although he was undoubtedly disappointed that they were so readily dismissed. What is remarkable in retrospect is that, given his knowledge of the community, he should not have predicted the reaction the tales would evoke. For London simply failed to anticipate just how unwilling these people were to let the rest of the world see society in Honolulu as it really was—how carefully they wished to shield themselves from the repugnant disease. London admired the stir Stevenson's "Damien Letters" created and remarked more than once that his stories would perhaps not be remembered half as long, but not for reasons like this... whatever his intentions when he wrote, it is doubly ironic that his basic sympathy for the problems that the caucasians of Hawaii faced should have been so misinterpreted. For all of his observations had not produced a true awareness, it seems, of the closed attitudes of most residents to the unpleasant. Not only did they shun any reference to leprosy, but most *kamaainas* were unwilling to admit that harmony had not been achieved among the races who had settled in the islands. Perhaps only a courageous outsider like London could risk the displeasure of the community leaders because he did not intend to settle in Paradise?

Yet the author was not all journalistic fervor, all angles and planes. His eye for a story was no less acute than the irony which struck the tone in these tales. And it is this running stream of wry humor which mellows the sometimes harsh subjects or issues he explores. Irony is the handy device London uses like a well-oiled hinge, yet perhaps too subtle was this tool for the Honolulu readers who first read the stories, who were still emotionally caught up in the fear of the disease, for it failed to reach the very audience he sought to capture!

London appears to be guilty, initially, of racial stereotyping in the story "Chun Ah Chun," it is true. At the onset, the character Chun is the classic Chinese merchant, who, having made good financially, marries into a local family to assure his place in society. The problem, when it arises, is probably what caused readers to assume that London was mocking Orientals. For Chun refuses to give up wearing his comfortable native garb despite the urging of his offspring. His solution emphasizes his intelligence (and London's appreciation for him as an individual character) when he deflects the attention his non-western habits have created by proceeding to marry off his admirable children, endowing them with generous settlements. With quiet assertiveness he offers solutions to problems which have plagued parents for centuries; this astute Chinese man demonstrates how to close the gap between the generations and the cultures at the same time. London expresses admiration for this man's spirit, for his persistence, for his sense of duty to his family as well as to himself.

In later years, critics were to compare London's style with giants like Hemingway, who openly acknowledged that he admired the author of these tales of the South Seas. Passages like: "Flesh is golden there. The native women are sun-ripe Junos; the native men bronzed Apollos." Here (in "Koolau the Leper") London presents an image of color; lush and tropical, yet simple and spare in its phrasing. The mellow tone points up the contrast between these tales and his stories of the North; the influence of his enviroment seems to have tempered the inflection, the harsher, sometimes brutal imagery of the past. London manages to maintain his earlier intensity and directness while introducing a tropical languor, softening his phrases without diminishing the simple forceful movement of his plots.

And simplicity is the vehicle which serves London well; within these clean, direct phrases he couches his wonderful irony, so that these yarns lose none of the color with which he invested them nearly eighty years ago. Now that the terror of leprosy is a thing of the past, now that his social sympathies have been re-asserted, we have only to enjoy London's ability to tell a good story, replete with admirable insights and rich imagery.

Miriam Rappolt
Kailua, Hawaii

Koolau The Leper

ecause we are sick they take away our liberty. We have obeyed the law. We have done no wrong. And yet they would put us in prison. Molokai is a prison. That you know. Niuli, there, his sister was sent to Molokai seven years ago. He has not seen her since. Nor will he ever see her. She must stay there until she dies. This is not her will. It is not Niuli's will. It is the will of the white men who rule the land. And who are these white men?

"We know. We have it from our fathers and our fathers' fathers. They came like lambs, speaking softly. Well might they speak softly, for we were many and strong, and all the islands were ours. As I say, they spoke softly. They were of two kinds. The one kind asked our permission, our gracious permission, to preach to us the word of God. The other kind asked our permission, our gracious permission, to trade with us. That was the beginning. To-day all the islands are theirs, all the land, all the cattle--everything is theirs. They that preached the word of God and they that preached the word of Rum have foregathered and become great chiefs. They live like kings in houses of many rooms with multitudes of servants to care for them. They who had nothing have everything, and if you, or I, or any Kanaka be hungry, they sneer and say, "Well, why don't you work? There are the plantations.' "

Koolau paused. He raised one hand, and with gnarled and twisted fingers lifted up the blazing wreath of hibiscus that crowned his black hair. The moonlight bathed the scene in silver. It was a night of peace, though those who sat about him and listened had all the seeming of battle-wrecks. Their faces were leonine. Here a space yawned in a face where should have been a nose, and there an arm-stump showed where a hand had rotted off. They were men and women beyond the pale, the thirty of them, for upon them had been placed the mark of the beast.

They sat, flower-garlanded, in the perfumed, luminous night, and their lips made uncouth noises and their throats rasped approval of Koolau's speech. They were creatures who once had been men and women. But they were men and women no longer. They were monsters--in face and form grotesque caricatures of everything human. They were hideously maimed and distorted, and had the seeming of creatures that had been racked in millenniums of hell. Their hands, when they possessed them, were like harpy-claws. Their faces were the misfits and slips, crushed and bruised by some mad god at play in the machinery of life. Here and there were features which the mad god had smeared half away, and one woman wept scalding tears from twin pits of horror, where her eyes once had been. Some were in pain and groaned from their chests. Others coughed, making sounds like the tearing of tissue. Two were idiots, more like huge apes marred in the making, until even an ape were an angel. They mowed and gibbered in the moonlight, under crowns of drooping, golden blossoms. One, whose bloated ear-lobe flapped like a fan upon his shoulder, caught up a gorgeous flower of orange and scarlet and with it decorated the monstrous ear that flip-flapped with his every movement.

And over these things Koolau was king. And this was his kingdom,—a flower-throttled gorge, with beetling cliffs and crags, from which floated the blattings of wild goats. On three sides the grim walls rose, festooned in fantastic draperies of tropic vegetation and pierced by cave-entrances—the rocky

lairs of Koolau's subjects. On the fourth side the earth fell a-
way into a tremendous abyss, and, far below, could be seen
the summits of lesser peaks and crags, at whose bases foamed
and rumbled the Pacific surge. In fine weather a boat could
land on the rocky beach that marked the entrance of Kalalau
Valley, but the weather must be very fine. And a cool-headed
mountaineer might climb from the beach to the head of Kalalau Valley, to this pocket among the peaks where Koolau
ruled; but such a mountaineer must be very cool of head, and
he must know the wild-goat trails as well. The marvel was
that the mass of human wreckage that constituted Koolau's
people should have been able to drag its helpless misery over
the giddy goat-trails to this inaccessible spot.

"Brothers," Koolau began.

But one of the mowing ape-like travesties emitted a wild
shriek of madness, and Koolau waited while the shrill ca-
chination was tossed back and forth among the rocky walls
and echoed distantly through the pulseless night.

"Brothers, is it not strange? Ours was the land, and behold, the land is not ours. What did these preachers of the
word of God and the word of Rum give us for the land? Have
you received one dollar, as much as one dollar, any one of
you, for the land? Yet it is theirs, and in return they tell us
we can go to work on the land, their land, and that what we
produce by our toil shall be theirs. Yet in the old days we did
not have to work. Also, when we are sick, they take away our
freedom."

"Who brought the sickness, Koolau?" demanded Kiloliana, a lean and wiry man with a face so like a laughing
faun's that one might expect to see the cloven hoofs under
him. They were cloven, it was true, but the cleavages were
great ulcers and livid putrefactions. Yet this was Kiloliana, the
most daring climber of them all, the man who knew every
goat-trail and who had led Koolau and his wretched followers
into the recesses of Kalalau.

"Ay, well questioned," Koolau answered. "Because we
would not work the miles of sugar-cane where once our
horses pastured, they brought the Chinese slaves from over
seas. And with them came the Chinese sickness--that which
we suffer from and because of which they would imprison us

on Molokai. We were born on Kauai. We have been to the
other islands, some here and some there, to Oahu, to Maui, to
Hawaii, to Honolulu. Yet always did we come back to Kauai.
Why did we come back? There must be a reason. Because we
love Kauai. We were born here. Here we have lived. And here
shall we die--unless--unless--there be weak hearts amongst us.
Such we do not want. They are fit for Molokai. And if there
be such, let them not remain. To-morrow the soldiers land on
the shore. Let the weak hearts go down to them. They will be
sent swiftly to Molokai. As for us, we shall stay and fight. But
know that we will not die. We have rifles. You know the narrow trails where men must creep, one by one. I, alone, Koolau who was once a cowboy on Niihau, can hold the trail
against a thousand men. Here is Kapalei, who was once a
judge over men and a man with honor, but who is now a
hunted rat, like you and me. Hear him. He is wise."

Kapalei arose. Once he had been a judge. He had gone
to college at Punahou. He had sat at meat with lords and chiefs
and the high representatives of alien powers who protected
the interests of traders and missionaries. Such had been Kapalei. But now, as Koolau had said, he was a hunted rat, a creature outside the law, sunk so deep in the mire of human horror that he was above the law as well as beneath it. His face
was featureless, save for gaping orifices and for the lidless
eyes that burned under hairless brows.

"Let us not make trouble," he began. "We ask to be left
alone. But if they do not leave us alone, then is the trouble
theirs, and the penalty. My fingers are gone, as you see." He
held up his stumps of hands that all might see. "Yet have I the
joint of one thumb left, and it can pull a trigger as firmly as
did its lost neighbor in the old days. We love Kauai. Let us
live here, or die here, but do not let us go to the prison of Molokai . The sickness is not ours. We have not sinned. The men
who preached the word of God and the word of Rum brought
the sickness with the coolie slaves who work the stolen land.
I have been a judge. I know the law and the justice, and I say
to you it is unjust to steal a man's land, to make that man sick
with the Chinese sickness, and then to put that man in prison
for life."

"Life is short, and the days are filled with pain," said

Koolau. "Let us drink and dance and be happy as we can."

From one of the rocky lairs calabashes were produced and passed around. The calabashes were filled with the fierce distillation of the root of the *ti*-plant; and as the liquid fire coursed through them and mounted to their brains, they forgot that they had once been men and women, for they were men and women once more. The woman who wept scalding tears from open eye-pits was indeed a woman apulse with life as she plucked the strings of an *ukulele* and lifted her voice in a barbaric love-call such as might have come from the dark forest-depths of the primeval world. The air tingled with her cry, softly imperious and seductive. Upon a mat, timing his rhythm to the woman's song, Kiloliana danced. It was unmistakable. Love danced in all his movements, and, next, dancing with him on the mat, was a woman whose heavy hips and generous breast gave the lie to her disease-corroded face. It was a dance of the living dead, for in their disintegrating bodies life still loved and longed. Ever the woman whose sightless eyes ran scalding tears chanted her love-cry, ever the dancers danced of love in the warm night, and ever the calabashes went around till in all their brains were maggots crawling of memory and desire. And with the woman on the mat danced a slender maid whose face was beautiful and unmarred, but whose twisted arms that rose and fell marked the disease's ravage. And the two idiots, gibbering and mouthing strange noises, danced apart, grotesque, fantastic, travestying love as they themselves had been travestied by life.

But the woman's love-cry broke midway, the calabashes were lowered, and the dancers ceased, as all gazed into the abyss above the sea, where a rocket flared like a wan phantom through the moonlit air.

"It is the soldiers," said Koolau. "Tomorrow there will be fighting. It is well to sleep and be prepared."

The lepers obeyed, crawling away to their lairs in the cliff, until only Koolau remained, sitting motionless in the moonlight, his rifle across his knees, as he gazed far down to the boats landing on the beach.

The far head of Kalalau Valley had been well chosen as a refuge. Except Kiloliana, who knew back-trails up the precipitous walls, no man could win to the gorge save by ad-

vancing across a knife-edged ridge. This passage was a hundred
yards in length. At best, it was a scant twelve inches wide. On
either side yawned the abyss. A slip, and to right or left
the man would fall to his death. But once across he would find
himself in an earthly paradise. A sea of vegetation laved the
landscape, pouring its green billows from wall to wall, dripping
from the cliff-lips in great vine-masses, and flinging a spray of
ferns and air-plants into the multitudinous crevices. During
the many months of Koolau's rule, he and his followers had
fought with this vegetable sea. The choking jungle, with its
riot of blossoms, had been driven back from the bananas,
oranges, and mangoes that grew wild. In little clearings grew
the wild arrow-root; on stone terraces, filled with soil scrap-
ings, were the *taro*-patches and the melons; and in every open
space where the sunshine penetrated, were *papaia*-trees
burdened with their golden fruit.

Koolau had been driven to this refuge from the lower
valley by the beach. And if he were driven from it in turn, he
knew of gorges among the jumbled peaks of the inner fast-
nesses where he could lead his subjects and live. And now he
lay with his rifle beside him, peering down through a tangled
screen of foliage at the soldiers on the beach. He noted that
they had large guns with them, from which the sunshine flashed
as from mirrors. The knife-edged passage lay directly before
him. Crawling upward along the trail that led to it he could see
tiny specks of men. He knew they were not the soldiers, but
the police. When they failed, then the soldiers would enter
the game.

He affectionately rubbed a twisted hand along his rifle-
barrel and made sure that the sights were clean. He had learned
to shoot as a wild-cattle hunter on Niihau, and on that island
his skill as a marksman was unforgotten. As the toiling specks
of men grew nearer and larger, he estimated the range, judged
the deflection of the wind that swept at right-angles across
the line of fire, and calibrated the chances of overshooting
marks that were so far below his level. But he did not shoot.
Not until they reached the beginning of the passage did he
make his presence known. He did not disclose himself, but
spoke from the thicket.

"What do you want?" he demanded.

"We want Koolau, the leper," answered the man who led the native police, himself a blue-eyed American.

"You must go back," Koolau said.

He knew the man, a deputy sheriff, for it was by him that he had been harried out of Niihau, across Kauai, to Kalalau Valley, and out of the valley to the gorge.

"Who are you?" the sheriff asked.

"I am Koolau, the leper," was the reply.

"Then come out. We want you. Dead or alive, there is a thousand dollars on your head. You cannot escape."

Koolau laughed aloud in the thicket.

"Come out!" the sheriff commanded, and was answered by silence.

He conferred with the police, and Koolau saw that they were preparing to rush him.

"Koolau," the sheriff called. "Koolau, I am coming across to get you."

"Then look first and well about you at the sun and sea and sky, for it will be the last time you behold them."

"That's all right, Koolau," the sheriff said soothingly. "I know you're a dead shot. But you won't shoot me. I have never done you any wrong."

Koolau grunted in the thicket.

"I say, you know, I've never done you any wrong, have I?" the sheriff persisted.

"You do me wrong when you try to put me in prison," was the reply. "And you do me wrong when you try for the thousand dollars on my head. If you will live, stay where you are."

"I've got to come across and get you. I'm sorry. But it is my duty."

"You will die before you get across."

The sheriff was no coward. Yet was he undecided. He gazed into the gulf on either side, and ran his eyes along the knife-edge he must travel. Then he made up his mind.

"Koolau," he called.

But the thicket remained silent.

"Koolau, don't shoot. I am coming."

The sheriff turned, gave some orders to the police, then started on his perilous way. He advanced slowly. It was like walking a tight rope. He had nothing to lean upon but the air. The lava-rock crumbled under his feet, and on either side the dislodged fragments pitched downward through the depths. The sun blazed upon him, and his face was wet with sweat. Still he advanced, until the halfway point was reached.

"Stop!" Koolau commanded from the thicket. "One more step and I shoot."

The sheriff halted, swaying for balance as he stood poised above the void. His face was pale, but his eyes were determined. He licked his dry lips before he spoke.

"Koolau, you won't shoot me. I know you won't."

He started once more. The bullet whirled him half-about. On his face was an expression of querulous surprise as he reeled to the fall. He tried to save himself by throwing his body across the knife-edge; but at that moment he knew death. The next moment the knife-edge was vacant. Then came the rush, five policemen, in single file, with superb steadiness, running along the knife-edge. At the same instant the rest of the posse opened fire on the thicket. It was madness. Five times Koolau pulled the trigger, so rapidly that his shots constituted a rattle. Changing his position and crouching low under the bullets that were biting and singing through the bushes, he peered out. Four of the police had followed the sheriff. The fifth lay across the knife-edge, still alive. On the farther side, no longer firing, were the surviving police. On the naked rock there was no hope for them. Before they could clamber down Koolau could have picked off the last man. But he did not fire, and, after a conference, one of them took off a white undershirt and waved it as a flag. Followed by another, he advanced along the knife-edge to their wounded comrade. Koolau gave no sign, but watched them slowly withdraw and become specks as they descended into the lower valley.

Two hours later, from another thicket, Koolau watched a body of police trying to make the ascent from the opposite side of the valley. He saw the wild goats flee before them as they climbed higher and higher, until he doubted his judgment and sent for Kiloliana who crawled in beside him.

"No, there is no way," said Kiloliana.

"The goats?" Koolau questioned.

"They come over from the next valley, but they cannot

pass to this. There is no way. Those men are not wiser than goats. They may fall to their deaths. Let us watch."

"They are brave men," said Koolau. 'Let us watch."

Side by side they lay among the morning-glories, with the yellow blossoms of the *hau* dropping upon them from overhead, watching the motes of men toil upward, till the thing happened, and three of them, slipping, rolling, sliding, dashed over a cliff-lip and fell sheer half a thousand feet.

Kiloliana chuckled.

"We will be bothered no more," he said.

"They have war-guns," Koolau made answer. "The soldiers have not yet spoken."

In the drowsy afternoon, most of the lepers lay in their rock dens asleep. Koolau, his rifle on his knees, fresh cleaned and ready, dozed in the entrance to his own den. The maid with the twisted arm lay below in the thicket and kept watch on the knife-edge passage. Suddenly Koolau was startled wide awake by the sound of an explosion on the beach. The next instant the atmosphere was incredibly rent asunder. The terrible sound frightened him. It was as if all the gods had caught the envelope of the sky in their hands and were ripping it apart as a woman rips apart a sheet of cotton cloth. But it was such an immense ripping, growing swiftly nearer. Koolau glanced up apprehensively, as if expecting to see the thing. Then high up on the cliff overhead the shell burst in a fountain of black smoke. The rock was shattered, the fragments falling to the foot of the cliff.

Koolau passed his hand across his sweaty brow. He was terribly shaken. He had had no experience with shell-fire, and this was more dreadful than anything he had imagined.

"One," said Kapahei, suddenly be-thinking himself to keep count.

A second and a third shell flew screaming over the top of the wall, bursting beyond view. Kapahei methodically kept the count. The lepers crowded into the open space before the caves. At first they were frightened, but as the shells continued their flight overhead the leper folk became reassured and began to admire the spectacle. The two idiots shrieked with delight, prancing wild antics as each air-tormenting shell went by. Koolau began to recover his confidence. No damage was being done. Evidently they could not aim such large missiles at such long range with the precision of a rifle.

But a change came over the situation. The shells began to fall short. One burst below in the thicket by the knife-edge. Koolau remembered the maid who lay there on watch, and ran down to see. The smoke was still rising from the bushes when he crawled in. He was astounded. The branches were splintered and broken. Where the girl had lain was a hole in the ground. The girl herself was in shattered fragments. The shell had burst right on her.

First peering out to make sure no soldiers were attempting the passage, Koolau started back on the run for the caves. All the time the shells were moaning, whining, screaming by, and the valley was rumbling and reverberating with the explosions. As he came in sight of the caves, he saw the two idiots cavorting about, clutching each other's hands with their stumps of finger. Even as he ran, Koolau saw a spout of black smoke rise from the ground, near to the idiots. They were flung apart bodily by the explosion. One lay motionless, but the other was dragging himself by his hands toward the cave. His legs trailed out helplessly behind him, while the blood was pouring from his body. He seemed bathed in blood, and as he crawled he cried like a little dog. The rest of the lepers, with the exception of Kapahei, had fled into the caves.

"Seventeen," said Kapahei. "Eighteen," he added.

This last shell had fairly entered into one of the caves. The explosion caused all the caves to empty. But from the particular cave no one emerged. Koolau crept in through the pungent, acrid smoke. Four bodies, frightfully mangled, lay about. One of them was the sightless woman whose tears till now had never ceased.

Outside, Koolau found his people in a panic and already beginning to climb the goat-trail that led out of the gorge and on among the jumbled heights and chasms. The wounded idiot whining feebly and dragging himself along on the ground by his hands, was trying to follow. But at the first pitch of the wall his helplessness overcame him and he fell back.

"It would be better to kill him," said Koolau to Kapahei, who still sat in the same place.

"Twenty-two," Kapahei answered. "Yes, it would be a wise thing to kill him. Twenty-three--twenty-four."

The idiot whined sharply when he saw the rifle leveled at him. Koolau hesitated, then lowered the gun.

"It is a hard thing to do," he said.

"You are a fool, twenty-six, twenty-seven," said Kapahei. "Let me show you."

He arose and, with a heavy fragment of rock in his hand, approached the wounded thing. As he lifted his arm to strike, a shell burst full upon him, relieving him of the necessity of the act and at the same time putting an end to his count.

Koolau was alone in the gorge. He watched the last of his people drag their crippled bodies over the brow of the height and disappear. Then he turned and went down to the thicket where the maid had been killed. The shell-fire still continued, but he remained; for far below he could see the soldiers climbing up. A shell burst twenty feet away. Flattening himself into the earth, he heard the rush of the fragments above his body. A shower of *hau* blossoms rained upon him. He lifted his head to peer down the trail, and sighed. He was very much afraid. Bullets from rifles would not have worried him, but this shell-fire was abominable. Each time a shell shrieked by he shivered and crouched; but each time he lifted his head again to watch the trail.

At last the shells ceased. This, he reasoned, was because the soldiers were drawing near. They crept along the trail in single file, and he tried to count them until he lost track. At any rate, there were a hundred or so of them--all come after Koolau the leper. He felt a fleeting prod of pride. With war guns and rifles, police and soldiers, they came for him, and he was only one man, a crippled wreck of a man at that. They offered a thousand dollars for him, dead or alive. In all his life he had never possessed that much money. The thought was a bitter one. Kapahei had been right. He, Koolau, had done no wrong. Because the *haoles* wanted labor with which to work the stolen land, they had brought in the Chinese coolies, and with them had come the sickness. And now, because he had caught the sickness, he was worth a thousand dollars—but not to himself. It was his worthless carcass, rotten with disease or dead from a bursting shell, that was worth all that money.

When the soldiers reached the knife-edged passage, he was prompted to warn them. But his gaze fell upon the body of the murdered maid, and he kept silent. When six had ventured on the knife-edge, he opened fire. Nor did he cease when the knife-edge was bare. He emptied his magazine, reloaded, and emptied it again. He kept on shooting. All his wrongs were blazing in his brain, and he was in a fury of vengeance. All down the goat-trail the soldiers were firing, and though they lay flat and sought to shelter themselves in the shallow in-equalities of the surface, they were exposed marks to him. Bullets whistled and thudded about him, and an occasional ricochet sang sharply through the air. One bullet ploughed a crease through his scalp, and a second burned across his shoulder-blade without breaking the skin.

It was a massacre, in which one man did the killing. The soldiers began to retreat, helping along their wounded. As Koolau picked them off he became aware of the smell of burnt meat. He glanced about him at first, and then discov-ered that it was his own hands. The heat of the rifle was do-ing it. The leprosy had destroyed most of the nerves in his hands. Though his flesh burned and he smelled it, there was no sensation.

He lay in the thicket, smiling, until he remembered the war guns. Without doubt they would open up on him again, and this time upon the very thicket from which he had in-flicted the damage. Scarcely had he changed his position to a nook behind a small shoulder of the wall where he had noted that no shells fell, than the bombardment recommenced. He counted the shells. Sixty more were thrown into the gorge before the warguns ceased. The tiny area was pitted with their explosions, until it seemed impossible that any creature could have survived. So the soldiers thought, for, under the burning afternoon sun, they climbed the goat-trail again. And again the knife-edged passage was disputed, and again they fell back to the beach.

For two days longer Koolau held the passage, though the soldiers contented themselves with flinging shells into his re-treat. Then Pahau, a leper boy, came to the top of the wall at the back of the gorge and shouted down to him that Kiloliana, hunting goats that they might eat, had been killed by a fall, and that the women were frightened and knew not what to do. Koolau called the boy down and left him with a spare gun with which to guard the passage. Koolau found his people disheartened. The majority of them were too helpless to forage food for themselves under such forbidding circumstances, and all were starving. He selected two women and a man who were not too far gone with the diesease, and sent them back to the gorge to bring up food and mats. The rest he cheered and consoled until even the weakest took a hand in building rough shelters for themselves.

But those he had dispatched for food did not return, and he started back for the gorge. As he came out on the brow of the wall, half a dozen rifles cracked. A bullet tore through the fleshy part of his shoulder, and his cheek was cut by a sliver of rock where a second bullet smashed against the cliff. In the moment that this happened, and he leaped back, he saw that the gorge was alive with soldiers. His own people had betrayed him. The shell-fire had been too terrible, and they had preferred the prison of Molokai.

Koolau dropped back and unslung one of his heavy cartridge-belts. Lying among the rocks, he allowed the head and shoulders of the first soldier to rise clearly into view before pulling trigger. Twice this happened, and then, after some delay, in place of a head and shoulders a white flag was thrust above the edge of the wall.

"What do you want?" he demanded.

"I want you, if you are Koolau the leper," came the answer.

Koolau forgot where he was, forgot everthing, as he lay and marvelled at the strange persistence of these *haoles* who would have their will though the sky fell in. Aye, they would have their will over all men and all things, even though they died in getting it. He could not but admire them, too, what of that will in them that was stronger than life and that bent all things to their bidding. He was convinced of the hopelessness of his struggle. There was no gainsaying that terrible will of the *haoles*. Though he killed a thousand, yet would they rise like the sands of the sea and come upon him, ever more and more. They never knew when they were beaten. That was their fault and their virtue. It was where his own kind lacked. He could see now, how the handful of the preachers of God and the preachers of Rum had conquered the land. It was because—

"Well, what have you got to say? Will you come with me?"

It was the voice of the invisible man under the white flag. There he was, like any *baole,* driving straight toward the end determined.

"Let us talk," said Koolau.

The man's head and shoulders arose, then his whole body. He was a smooth-faced, blue-eyed youngster of twenty-five, slender and natty in his captain's uniform. He advanced until halted, then seated himself a dozen feet away:—

"You are a brave man," said Koolau wonderingly. "I could kill you like a fly."

"No, you couldn't," was the answer.

"Why not?"

"Because you are a man, Koolau, though a bad one. I know your story. You kill fairly."

Koolau grunted, but was secretly pleased.

"What have you done with my people?" he demanded. "The boy, the two women, and the man?"

"They gave themselves up, as I have now come for you to do."

Koolau laughed incredulously.

"I am a free man," he announced. "I have done no wrong. All I ask is to be left alone. I have lived free, and I shall die free. I will never give myself up."

"Then your people are wiser than you," answered the young captain. "Look—they are coming now."

Koolau turned and watched the remnant of his band approach. Groaning and sighing, a ghastly procession, it dragged its wretchedness past. It was given to Koolau to taste a deeper bitterness, for they hurled imprecations and insults at him as they went by; and the panting hag who brought up the rear halted, and with skinny, harpy-claws extended, shaking her snarling death's head from side to side, she laid a curse upon him. One by one they dropped over the lip-edge and surrendered to the hiding soldiers.

"You can go now," said Koolau to the captain. "I will never give myself up. That is my last word. Good-by."

The captian slipped over the cliff to his soldiers. The next moment, and without a flag of truce, he hoisted his hat on his scabbard, and Koolau's bullet tore through it. That afternoon they shelled him out from the beach, and as he retreated into the high inaccessible pockets beyond, the soldiers followed him.

For six weeks they hunted him from pocket to pocket, over the volcanic peaks and along the goat-trails. When he hid in the lantana jungle, they formed lines of beaters, and through lantana jungle and guava scrub they drove him like a rabbit. But ever he turned and doubled and eluded. There was no cornering him. When pressed too closely, his sure rifle held them back and they carried their wounded down the goat trails to the beach. There were times when they did the shooting as his brown body showed for a moment through the underbrush. Once, five of them caught him on an exposed goat-trail between pockets. They emptied their rifles at him as he limped and climbed along his dizzy way. Afterward they found blood-stains and knew that he was wounded. At the end of six weeks they gave up. The soldiers and police returned to Honolulu, and Kalalau Valley was left to him for his own, though head-hunters ventured after him from time to time and to their own undoing.

Two years later, and for the last time, Koolau crawled into a thicket and lay down among the *ti*-leaves and wild ginger blossoms. Free he had lived, and free he was dying. A slight drizzle of rain began to fall, and he drew a ragged blanket about the distorted wreck of his limbs. His body was covered with an oilskin coat. Across his chest he laid his Mauser rifle, lingering affectionately for a moment to wipe the dampness from the barrel. The hand with which he wiped had no fingers left upon it with which to pull the trigger.

He closed his eyes, for, from the weakness in his body and the fuzzy turmoil in his brain, he knew that his end was near. Like a wild animal he had crept into hiding to die. Half-conscious, aimless and wandering, he lived back in his life to his early manhood on Niihau. As life faded and the drip of the rain grew dim in his ears, it seemed to him that he was once more in the thick of the horse-breaking, with raw colts rearing and bucking under him, his stirrups tied together beneath, or charging madly about the breaking corral and driving the helping cowboys over the rails. The next instant, and with seeming naturalness, he found himself pursuing the wild bulls of the upland pastures, roping them and leading them down to the valleys. Again the sweat and dust of the branding pen stung his eyes and bit his nostrils.

All his lusty, whole-bodied youth was his, until the sharp pangs of impending dissolution brought him back. He lifted his monstrous hands and gazed at them in wonder. But how? Why? Why should the wholeness of that wild youth of his change to this? Then he remembered, and once again, and for a moment, he was Koolau, the leper. His eyelids fluttered wearily down and the drip of the rain ceased in his ears. A prolonged trembling set up in his body. This, too, ceased. He half-lifted his head, but it fell back. Then his eyes opened, and did not close. His last thought was of his Mauser, and he pressed it against his chest with his folded, fingerless hands. So passed Koolau, the leper.

The House of Pride

ERCIVAL FORD wondered why he had come. He did not dance. He did not care much for army people. Yet he knew them all—gliding and revolving there on the broad *lanai* of the Seaside, the officers in their fresh-starched uniforms of white, the civilians in white and black, and the women bare of shoulders and arms. After two years in Honolulu the Twentieth was departing to its new station in Alaska, and Percival Ford, as one of the big men of the Islands, could not help knowing the officers and their women.

But between knowing and liking was a vast gulf. The army women frightened him just a little. They were in ways quite different from the women he liked best—the elderly women, the spinsters and the bespectacled maidens, and very serious women of all ages whom he met on church and library and kindergarten committees, who came meekly to him for contributions and advice. He ruled those women by virtue of his superior mentality, his great wealth, and the high place he occupied in the commercial baronage of Hawaii. And he was not afraid of them in the least. Sex, with them, was not obtrusive. Yes, that was it. There was in them something else, or more, than the assertive grossness of life. He was fastidious; he acknowledge that to himself; and these army women, with their bare shoulders and naked arms, their straight-looking eyes, their vitality and challenging femaleness, jarred upon his sensibilities.

Nor did he get on better with the army men, who took life lightly, drinking and smoking and swearing their way through life and asserting the essential grossness of flesh no less shamelessly than their women. He was always uncomfortable in the company of the army men. They seemed uncomfortable, too. And he felt, always, that they were laughing at him up their sleeves, or pitying him, or tolerating him. Then, too, they seemed, by mere contiguity, to emphasize a lack in him, to call attention to that in them which he did not possess and which he thanked God he did not possess. Faugh! They were like their women!

In fact, Percival Ford was no more a woman's man than he was a man's man. A glance at him told the reason. He had a good constitution, never was on intimate terms with sickness, nor even mild disorders; but he lacked vitality. His was a negative organism. No blood with a ferment in it could have nourished and shaped that long and narrow face, those thin lips, lean cheeks, and the small sharp eyes. The thatch of hair, dust-colored, straight and sparse, advertised the niggard soil, as did the nose, thin, delicately modeled, and just hinting the suggestion of a beak. His meagre blood had denied him much of life, and permitted him to be an extremist in one thing only, which thing was righteousness. Over right conduct he pondered and agonized, and that he should do right was as necessary to his nature as loving and being loved were necessary to commoner clay.

He was sitting under the algaroba trees between the *lanai* and the beach. His eyes wandered over the dancers and he turned his head away and gazed seaward across the mellow-sounding surf to the Southern Cross burning low on the horizon. He was irritated by the bare shoulders and arms of the women. If he had a daughter he would never permit it, never. But his hypothesis was the sheerest abstraction. The thought process had been accompanied by no inner vision of that daughter. He did not see a daughter with arms and shoulders.

Instead, he smiled at the remote contingency of marriage. He was thirty-five, and, having no personal experience of love, he looked upon it, not as mythical, but as bestial. Anybody could marry. The Japanese and Chinese coolies, toiling on the sugar plantaions and in the rice-fields, married. They invariably married at the first opportunity. It was because they were so low in the scale of life. There was nothing else for them to do. They were like the army men and women. But for him there were other and higher things. He was different from them—from all of them. He was proud of how he happened to be. He had come of no petty love-match. He had come of lofty conception of duty and of devotion to a cause. His father had not married for love. Love was a madness that had never perturbed Isaac Ford. When he answered the call to go to the heathen with the message of life, he had had no thought and no desire for marriage. In this they were alike, his father and he. But the Board of Missions was economical. With New England thrift it weighed and measured and decided that married missionaries were less expensive per capita and more efficacious. So the Board commanded Isaac Ford to marry. Futhermore, it furnished him with a wife, another zealous soul with no thought of marriage, intent only on doing the Lord's work among the heathen. They saw each other for the first time in Boston. The Board brought them together, arranged everything, and by the end of the week they were married and started on the long voyage around the Horn.

Percival Ford was proud that he had come of such a union. He had been born high, and he thought of himself as a spiritual aristocrat. And he was proud of his father. It was a passion with him. The erect, austere figure of Isaac Ford had burned itself upon his pride. On his desk was a miniature of that soldier of the Lord. In his bedroom hung the portrait of Isaac Ford, painted at the time when he had served under the Monarchy as prime minister. Not that Isaac Ford had coveted place and worldly wealth, but that, as prime minister, and later, as banker, he had been of greater service to the missionary cause. The German crowd, and the English crowd, and all the rest of the trading crowd, had sneered at Isaac Ford as a commercial soul-saver, but he, his son, knew different. When the natives, emerging abruptly from their feudal system, with no conception of the nature and significance of property in land, were letting their broad acres slip through their fingers, it was Isaac Ford who had stepped in between the trading crowd and its prey and taken possesion of fat, vast holdings. Small wonder the trading crowd did not like his memory. But he had never looked upon his enormous wealth as his own. He had considered himself God's steward. Out of the revenues he had built schools, and hospitals, and churches. Nor was it his fault that sugar, after the slump, had paid forty per cent; that the bank he founded had prospered into a railroad; and that, among other things, fifty thousand acres of Oahu pasture land, which he had bought for a dollar an acre, grew eight tons of sugar to the acre every eighteen months. No, in all truth Isaac Ford was an heroic figure, fit, so Percival Ford thought privately, to stand beside the statue of Kamehamaha I in front of the Judiciary Building. Isaac Ford was gone, but he, his son, carried on the good work at least as inflexibly if not as masterfully.

He turned his eyes back to the *lanai*. What was the difference, he asked himself, between the shameless, grass-girdled *hula* dances and the décolleté dances of the women of his own race? Was there an essential difference? or was it a matter of degree?

As he pondered the problem a hand rested on his shoulder.

"Hello, Ford, what are you doing here? Isn't this a bit festive?"

"I try to be lenient, Dr. Kennedy, even as I look on," Percival Ford answered gravely. "Won't you sit down?"

Dr. Kennedy sat down, clapping his palms sharply. A white-clad Japanese servant answered swiftly.

Scotch and soda was Kennedy's order; then, turning to the other, he said:

"Of course, I don't ask you."

"But I will take something," Ford said firmly. The doctor's eyes showed surprise, and the servant waited. "Boy, a lemonade, please."

The doctor laughed at it heartily, as a joke on himself, and glanced at the musicians under the *hau* tree.

"Why, it's the Aloha Orchestra," he said. "I thought they

were with the Hawaiian Hotel on Tuesday nights. Some rumpus, I guess."

His eyes paused for a moment and dwelt upon the one
who was playing a guitar and singing a Hawaiian song to the
accompaniment of all the instruments. His face became
grave as he looked at the singer, and it was still grave as he
turned it to his companion.

"Look here, Ford, isn't it time you let up on Joe Garland? I understand you are in opposition to the Promotion
Committee's sending him to the States on this surf-board pro-
position, and I've been wanting to speak to you about it.
I should have thought you'd be glad to get him out of the
country. It would be a good way to end your persecution of
him."

"Persecution?" Percival Ford's eyebrows lifted in-
terrogatively.

"Call it by any name you please," Kennedy went on.
"You've hounded that poor devil for years. It's not his
fault. Even you will admit that."

"Not his fault?" Percival Ford's thin lips drew tightly
together for the moment. "Joe Garland is dissolute and idle.
He has always been a wastrel, a profligate."

"But that's no reason you should keep on after him the
way you do. I've watched you from the beginning. The first
thing you did when you returned from college and found him
working on the plantation as outside *luna* was to fire him—you
with your millions, and he with his sixty dollars a month."

"Not the first thing," Percival Ford said judicially, in
the tone he was accustomed to use in committee meetings.
"I gave him his warning. The superintendent said he was a
capable *luna*. I had no objection to him on that ground. It
was what he did outside working hours. He undid my work
faster than I could build it up. Of what use were the Sunday
schools, the night schools, and the sewing classes, when in the
evenings there was Joe Garland with his infernal and eternal
tum-tumming of guitar and *ukulele*, his strong drink, and his
hula dancing? After I warned him, I came upon him—I shall
never forget it—came upon him, down at the cabins. It was
evening. I could hear the *hula* songs before I saw the scene.
And when I did see it, there were the girls, shameless in the

moonlight and dancing—the girls upon whom I had worked to teach clean living and right conduct. And there were three girls there, I remember, just graduated from the mission school. Of course I discharged Joe Garland. I know it was the same at Hilo. People said I went out of my way when I per-suaded Mason and Fitch to discharge him. But it was the miss-ionaries who requested me to do so. He was undoing their work by his reprehensible example."

Afterwards, when he got on the railroad, your railroad, he was discharged without cause," Kennedy challenged.

"Not so," was the quick answer. "I had him into my private office and talked with him for half an hour."

"You discharged him for inefficiency?"

"For immoral living, if you please."

Dr. Kennedy laughed with a grating sound. "Who the devil gave it to you to be judge and jury? Does landlordism give you control of the immortal souls of those that toil for you? I have been your physician. Am I to expect to-morrow your ukase that I give up Scotch and soda or your patronage? Bah! Ford, you take life too seriously. Besides, when Joe got into that smuggling scrape (he wasn't in your employ, either), and he sent word to you, asked you to pay his fine, you left him to do his six months hard labor on the reef. Don't forget, you left Joe Garland in the lurch that time. You threw him down, hard; and yet I remember the first day you came to school—we boarded, you were only a day scholar. You had to be initiated. Three times under in the swimming tank—you re-member, it was the regular dose every new boy got. And you held back. You denied that you could swim. You were fright-ened, hysterical—"

"Yes, I know," Percival Ford said slowly. "I was fright-ened. And it was a lie, for I could swim. . . . And I was fright-ened."

"And you remember who fought for you? who lied for you harder than you could lie and swore he knew you couldn't swim? Who jumped into the tank and pulled you out after the first under and was nearly drowned for it by the other boys, who had discovered by that time that you *could* swim?"

"Of course I know," the other rejoined coldly. "But a

generous act as a boy does not excuse a lifetime of wrong living."

"He has never done wrong to you?—personally and directly, I mean?"

"No," was Percival Ford's answer. "That is what makes my position impregnable. I have no personal spite against him. He is bad, that is all. His life is bad—"

"Which is another way of saying that he does not agree with you in the way life should be lived," the doctor interrupted.

"Have it that way. It is immaterial. He is an idler—"

"With reason," was the interuption "considering the jobs out of which you have knocked him."

"He is immoral—"

"Oh, hold on now, Ford. Don't go harping on that. You are pure New England stock. Joe Garland is half Kanaka. Your blood is thin. His is warm. Life is one thing to you, another thing to him. He laughs and sings and dances through life, genial, unselfish, childlike, everybody's friend. You go through life like a perambulating prayer-wheel, a friend of nobody but the righteous, and the righteous are those who agree with you as to what is right. And after all, who shall say? You live like an anchorite. Joe Garland lives like a good fellow. Who has extracted the most from life? We are paid to live, you know. When the wages are too meagre we throw up the job, which is the cause, believe me, of all rational suicide. Joe Garland would starve to death on the wages you get from life. You see, he is made differently. So would you starve on his wages, which are singing, and love—"

"Lust, if you will pardon me," was the interruption.

Dr. Kennedy smiled.

"Love, to you, is a word of four letters and a definition which you have extracted from the dictionary. But love, real love, dewy and palpitant and tender you do not know. If God made you and me, and men and women, believe me he made love, too. But to come back. It's about time you quit hounding Joe Garland. It is not worthy of you, and it is cowardly. The thing for you to do is to reach out and lend him a hand."

"Why I, any more than you?" the other demanded. "Why don't you reach him a hand?"

"I have. I'm reaching him a hand now. I'm trying to get you not to down the Promotion Committee's propostion of sending him away. I got him the job at Hilo with Mason and Fitch. I've got him half a dozen jobs, out of every one of which you drove him. But never mind that. Don't forget one thing— and a little frankness won't hurt you—it is not fair play to saddle another's fault on Joe Garland; and you know that you, least of all, are the man to do it. Why, man, it's not good taste. It's positively indecent."

"Now I don't follow you," Percival Ford answered. "You're up in the air with some obscure scientific theory of heredity and personal irresponsibility. But how any theory can hold Joe Garland irresponsible for his wrongdoings and at the same time hold me personally responsible for them—more responsible than any one else, including Joe Garland—is beyond me."

"It's a matter of delicacy, I suppose, or of taste, that prevents you from following me," Dr. Kennedy snapped out. "It's all very well, for the sake of society, tacitly to ignore some things, but you do more than tacitly ignore."

"What is it, pray, that I tacitly ignore!"

Dr. Kennedy was angry. A deeper red than that of constitutional Scotch and soda suffused his face, as he answered:

"Your father's son."

"Now just what do you mean?"

"Damn it, man, you can't ask me to be plainer-spoken than that. But if you will, all right—Isaac's Ford's son—Joe Garland—your brother."

Percival Ford sat quietly, an annoyed and shocked expression on his face. Kennedy looked at him curiously, then, as the slow minutes dragged by, became embarrassed and frightened.

"My God!" he cried finally, "you don't mean to tell me that you didn't know!"

As in answer, Percival Ford's cheeks turned slowly gray.

"It's a ghastly joke," he said, "a ghastly joke."

The doctor had got himself in hand.

"Everybody knows it," he said. "I thought you knew it.

And since you don't know it, it's time you did, and I'm glad of the chance of setting you straight. Joe Garland and you are brothers—half-brothers."

"It's a lie," Ford cried. "You don't mean it. Joe Garland's mother was Eliza Kunilio." (Dr. Kennedy nodded.) "I remember her well, with her duck pond and *taro* patch. His father was Joseph Garland, the beach-comber." (Dr. Kennedy shook his head.) "He died only two or three years ago. He used to get drunk. There's where Joe got his dissoluteness. There's the heredity for you."

"And nobody told you," Kennedy said wonderingly, after a pause.

"Dr. Kennedy, you have said something terrible, which I cannot allow to pass. You must either prove or, or ..."

"Prove it yourself. Turn around and look at him. You've got him in profile. Look at his nose. That's Isaac Ford's. Yours is a thin edition of it. That's right. Look. The lines are fuller, but they are all there."

Percival Ford looked at the Kanaka half-breed who played under the *hau* tree, and it seemed, as by some illumination, that he was gazing on a wraith of himself. Feature after feature flashed up an unmistakable resemblance. Or, rather, it was he who was the wraith of that other full-muscled and generously moulded man. And his features, and that other man's features, were all reminiscent of Isaac Ford. And nobody had told him. Every line of Isaac Ford's face he knew. Miniatures, protraits, and photographs of his father were passing in review through his mind, and here and there, over and again, in the face before him, he caught resemblances and vague hints of likeness. It was devil's work that could reproduce the austere features of Isaac Ford in the loose and sensuous features before him. Once, the man turned, and for one flashing instant it seemed to Percival Ford that he saw his father, dead and gone, peering at him out of the face of Joe Garland.

"It's nothing at all," he could faintly hear Dr. Kennedy saying. "They were all mixed up in the old days. You know that. You've seen it all your life. Sailors married queens and begat princesses and all the rest of it. It was the usual thing in the Islands."

"But not with my father," Percival Ford interrupted.

"There you are." Kennedy shrugged his shoulders. "Cosmic sap and smoke of life. Old Isaac Ford was straight-laced and all the rest, and I know there's no explaining it, least of all to himself. He understood it no more than you do. Smoke of life, that's all. And don't forget one thing, Ford. There was a dab of unruly blood in old Isaac Ford, and Joe Garland inherited it—all of it, smoke of life and cosmic sap; while you inherited all of old Isaac's ascetic blood. And just because your blood is cold, well-ordered, and well-disciplined, is no reason that you should frown upon Joe Garland. When Joe Garland undoes the work you do, remember that it is only old Isaac Ford on both sides, undoing with one hand what he does with the other. You are Isaac Ford's right hand, let us say; Joe Garland is his left hand."

Percival Ford made no answer, and in the silence Dr. Kennedy finished his forgotten Scotch and soda. From across the grounds an automobile hooted imperatively.

"There's the machine," Dr. Kennedy said, rising. "I've got to run. I'm sorry I've shaken you up, and at the same time I'm glad. And know one thing, Isaac Ford's dab of unruly blood was remarkably small, and Joe Garland got it all. And one other thing. If your father's left hand offend you, don't smite it off. Besides, Joe is all right. Frankly, if I could choose between you and him to live with me on a desert isle, I'd choose Joe."

Little bare-legged children ran about him, playing, on the grass; but Percival Ford did not see them. He was gazing steadily at the singer under the *hau* tree. He even changed his position once, to get closer. The clerk of the Seaside went by, limping with age and dragging his reluctant feet: He had lived forty years on the Islands. Percival Ford beckoned to him, and the clerk came respecfully, and wondering that he should be noticed by Percival Ford.

"John," Ford said, "I want you to give me some information. Won't you sit down?"

The clerk sat down awkwardly, stunned by the unexpected honor. He blinked at the other and mumbled, "Yes, sir, thank you."

"John, who is Joe Garland?"

The clerk stared at him, blinked, cleared his throat, and said nothing.

"Go on," Percival Ford commanded. "Who is he?"

"You're joking me, sir," the other managed to articulate.

"I spoke to you seriously."

The clerk recoiled from him.

"You don't mean to say you don't know?" he questioned, his question in itself the answer.

"I want to know."

"Why, he's—" John broke off and looked about him helplessly. "Hadn't you better ask somebody else? Everybody thought you knew. We always thought . . ."

"Yes, go ahead."

"We always thought that that was why you had it in for him."

Photographs and miniatures of Isaac Ford were trooping through his son's brain, and ghosts of Isaac Ford seemed in the air about him. "I wish you good night, sir," he could hear the clerk saying, and he saw him beginning to limp away.

"John," he called abruptly.

John came back and stood near him, blinking and nervously moistening his lips.

"You haven't told me yet, you know."

"Oh, about Joe Garland?"

"Yes, about Joe Garland. Who is he?"

"He's your brother, sir, if I say it who shouldn't."

"Thank you, John. Good night."

"And you didn't know?" the old man queried, content to linger, now that the crucial point was past.

"Thank you, John. Good night," was the response.

"Yes, sir, thank you, sir. I think it's going to rain. Good night, sir."

Out of a clear sky, filled only with stars and moonlight, fell a rain so fine and attenuated as to resemble a vapor-spray. Nobody minded it; the children played on, running bare-legged over the grass and leaping into the sand; and in a few minutes it was gone. In the south-east, Diamond Head, a black blot, sharply defined, silhouetted its crater-form against the stars. At sleepy intervals the surf flung its foam across the sand to the grass, and far out could be seen the black specks of swimmers under the moon. The voices of the singers, singing a waltz, died away; and in the silence, from somewhere under the trees, arose the laugh of a woman that was a love-cry. It startled Percival Ford, and it reminded him of Dr. Kennedy's phrase. Down by the outrigger canoes, where they lay hauled out on the sand, he saw men and women, Kanakas, reclining languorously, like lotus-eaters, the women in white *holokus;* and against one such *holoku* he saw the dark head of the steersman of the canoe resting upon the woman's shoulder. Farther down, where the strip of sand widened at the entrance to the lagoon, he saw a man and woman walking side by side. As they drew near the light *lanai,* he saw the woman's hand go down to her waist and disengage a girdling arm. And as they passed him, Percival Ford nodded to a captain he knew, and to a major's daughter. Smoke of life, that was it, an ample phrase. And again, from under the dark algaroba trees arose the laugh of a woman that was a love-cry; and past his chair, on the way to bed, a bare-legged youngster was led by a chiding Japanese nurse-maid. The voices of the singers broke softly and meltingly into an Hawaiian love song, and officers and women, with encircling arms, were gliding and whirling on the *lanai;* and once again the woman laughed under the algaroba trees.

And Percival Ford knew only disapproval of it all. He was irritated by the love-laugh of the woman, by the steersman with pillowed head on the white *holoku,* by the couples that walked on the beach, by the officers and women that danced, and by the voices of the singers singing of love, and his brother singing there with them under the *hau* tree. The woman that laughed expecially irritated him. A curious train of thought was aroused. He was Isaac Ford's son, and what had happened with Isaac Ford might happen with him. He felt in his cheeks the faint heat of a blush at the thought, and experienced a poignant sense of shame. He was appalled by what was in his blood. It was like learning suddenly that his father had been a leper and that his own blood might bear the taint of that dread disease. Isaac Ford, the austere soldier of the Lord—the old hypocrite! What difference between him and any beach-comber? The house of pride that Percival Ford had builded was tumbling about his ears.

The hours passed, the army people laughed and danced, the native orchestra played on, and Percival Ford wrestled with the abrupt and overwhelming problem that had been thrust upon him. He prayed quietly, his elbow on the table, his head bowed upon his hand, with all the appearance of any tired onlooker. Between the dances the army men and women and the civilians fluttered up to him and buzzed conventionally, and when they went back to the *lanai* he took up his wrestling where he had left it off.

He began to patch together his shattered ideal of Isaac Ford, and for cement he used a cunning and subtle logic. It was of the sort that is compounded in the brain laboratories of egotists, and it worked. It was incontrovertible that his father had been made of finer clay than those about him; but still, old Isaac had been only in the process of becoming, while he, Percival Ford, had become. As proof of it, he rehabilitated his father and at the same time exalted himself. His lean little ego waxed to colossal proportions. He was great enough to forgive. He glowed at the thought of it. Isaac Ford had been great, but he was greater, for he could forgive Isaac Ford and even restore him to the holy place in his memory, though the place was not quite so holy as it had been. Also, he applauded Isaac Ford for having ignored the outcome of his one step aside. Very well, he too, would ignore it.

The dance was breaking up. The orchestra had finished "Aloha Oe" and was preparing to go home. Percival Ford clapped his hands for the Japanese servant.

"You tell that man I want to see him," he said pointing out Joe Garland. "Tell him come here, now."

Joe Garland approached and halted respectfully several paces away, nervously fingering the guitar which he still carried. The other did not ask him to sit down.

"You are my brother," he said.

"Why, everybody knows that," was the reply, in tones of wonderment.

"Yes, so I understand," Percival Ford said dryly. "But I did not know it till this evening."

The half-brother waited uncomfortably in the silence

that followed, during which Percival Ford coolly considered his next utterance.

"You remember that first time I came to school and the boys ducked me? " he asked. "Why did you take my part?"

The half-brother smiled bashfully.

"Because you knew?"

"Yes, that was why."

"But I didn't know," Percival Ford said in the same dry fashion.

"Yes," the other said.

Another silence fell. Servants were beginning to put out the lights on the *lanai.*

"You know . . . now," the half brother said simply.

Percival Ford frowned. Then he looked the other over with a considering eye.

"How much will you take to leave the Islands and never come back?" he demanded.

"And never come back?" Joe Garland faltered. "It is the only land I know. Other lands are cold. I do not know other lands. I have many friends here. In other lands there would not be one voice to say, '*Aloha,* Joe, my boy.' "

"I said never to come back," Percival Ford reiterated. "The *Alameda* sails to-morrow for San Francisco."

Joe Garland was bewildered.

"But why?" he asked. "You know now that we are brothers."

"That is why," was the retort. "As you said yourself, everybody knows. I will make it worth your while."

All the awkwardness and embarrassment disappeared from Joe Garland. Birth and station were bridged and reversed.

"You want me to go?" he demanded.

"I want you to go and never to come back," Percival Ford answered.

And in that moment, flashing and fleeting, it was given him to see his brother tower above him like a mountain, and to feel himself dwindle and dwarf to microscopic insignificance. But it is not well for one to see himself truly, nor can one so see himself for long and live; and only for that flashing moment did Percival Ford see himself and his brother in true perspective. The next moment he was mastered by his meagre and insatiable ego.

"As I said, I will make it worth your while. You will not suffer. I will pay you well."

"All right," Joe Garland said. "I'll go."

He started to turn away.

"Joe," the other called. "You see my lawyer to-morrow morning. Five hundred down and two hundred a month as long as you stay away."

"You are very kind," Joe Garland answered softly. "You are too kind. And anyway, I guess I don't want your money. I go to-morrow on the *Alameda.*"

He walked away, but did not say good-by.

Percival Ford clapped his hands.

"Boy," he said to the Japanese, "a lemonade."

And over the lemonade he smiled long and contentedly to himself.

Chun Ah Chun

THERE WAS nothing striking in the appearence of Chun
Ah Chun. He was rather undersized, as Chinese go, and
the Chinese narrow shoulders and spareness of flesh
were his. The average tourist, casually glimpsing him on the
streets of Honolulu, would have concluded that he was a good-
natured little Chinese, probably the proprietor of a prosperous
laundry or tailorshop. In so far as good nature and prosperity
went, the judgment would be correct, though beneath the mark;
for Ah Chun was as good-natured as he was prosperous, and
of the latter no man knew a tithe the tale. It was well known
that he was enormously wealthy, but in his case "enormous"
was merely the symbol for the unknown.

Ah Chun had shrewd little eyes, black and beady and so
very little that they were like gimlet holes. But they were wide
apart, and they sheltered under a forehead that was patently
the forehead of a thinker. For Ah Chun had his problems, and
had had them all his life.—Not that he ever worried over them.
He was essentially a philosopher, and whether as coolie, or
multi-millionaire and master of many men, his poise of soul
was the same. He lived always in the high equanimity of spiritu-

al repose, undeterred by good fortune, unruffled by ill fortune.
All things went well with him, whether they were blows from
the overseer in the cane field or a slump in the price of sugar
when he owned those cane fields himself. Thus, from the stead-
fast rock of his sure content he mastered problems such as are
given to few men to consider, much less to a Chinese peasant.

He was precisely that—a Chinese peasant, born to labor
in the fields all his days like a beast, but fated to escape from
the fields like the prince in a fairy tale. Ah Chun did not remember his father, a small farmer in a district not far from
Canton; nor did he remember much of his mother, who had
died when he was six. But he did remember his respected uncle,
Ah Kow, for him had he served as a slave from his sixth year to
his twenty-fourth. It was then that he escaped by contracting
himself as a coolie to labor for three years on the sugar plantations of Hawaii for fifty cents a day.

Ah Chun was observant. He perceived little details that
not one man in a thousand ever noticed. Three years he worked
in the field, at the end of which time he knew more about cane-
growing than the overseers or even the superintendent, while
the superintendent would have been astounded at the knowledge the weazened little coolie possessed of the reduction processes in the mill. But Ah Chun did not study only sugar processes. He studied to find out how men came to be owners of
sugar mills and plantations. One judgment he achieved early,
namely, that men did not become rich from the labor of their
own hands. He knew, for he had labored for a score of years
himself. The men who grew rich did so from the labor of the
hands of others. That man was richest who had the greatest
number of his fellow creatures toiling for him.

So, when his term of contract was up, Ah Chun invested
his savings in a small importing store, going into partnership
with one, Ah Yung. The firm ultimately became the great one
of "Ah Chun & Ah Yung," which handled anything from India
silks and ginseng to guano islands and blackbird brigs. In the
meantime, Ah Chun hired out as cook. He was a good cook,
and in three years he was the highest paid chef in Honolulu.
His career was assured, and he was a fool to abandon it, as
Dantin, his employer, told him; but Ah Chun knew his own
mind best, and for knowing it was called a triple-fool and given

a present of fifty dollars over and above the wages due him.

The firm of Ah Chun & Ah Yung was prospering. There was no need for Ah Chun longer to be a cook. There were boom times in Hawaii. Sugar was being extensively planted, and labor was needed. Ah Chun saw the chance, and went into the labor-importing business. He brought thousands of Cantonese coolies into Hawaii, and his wealth began to grow. He made investments. His beady black eyes saw bargains where other men saw bankruptcy. He bought a fish-pond for a song, which later paid five hundred per cent and was the opening wedge by which he monopolized the fish market of Honolulu. He did not talk for publication, nor figure in politics, nor play at revolutions, but he forecast events more clearly and farther ahead than did the men who engineered them. In his mind's eye he saw Honolulu a modern, electric-lighted city at a time when it straggled, unkempt and sand-tormented, over a barren reef of uplifted coral rock. So he bought land. He bought land from merchants who needed ready cash, from impecunious natives, from riotous traders' sons, from widows and orphans and the lepers deported to Molokai; and, somehow, as the years went by, the pieces of land he had bought proved to be needed for warehouses, or office buildings, or hotels. He leased, and rented, sold and bought, and resold again.

But there were other things as well. He put his confidence and his money into Parkinson, the renegade captain whom nobody would trust. And Parkinson sailed away on mysterious little voyages in the little *Vega*. Parkinson was taken care of until he died, and years afterward Honolulu was astonished when the news leaked out that the Drake and Acorn guano islands had been sold to the British Phosphate Trust for three-quarters of a million. Then there were the fat, lush days of King Kalakaua, when Ah Chun paid three hundred thousand dollars for the opium license. If he paid a third of a million for the drug monopoly, the investment was nevertheless a good one, for the dividends bought him the Kalalau Plantation, which, in turn, paid him thirty per cent for seventeen years and was ultimately sold by him for a million and a half.

It was under the Kamehamehas, long before, that he had served his own country as Chinese Consul—a position that was not altogether unlucrative; and it was under Kamehameha IV.

that he changed his citizenship, becoming an Hawaiian subject in order to marry Stella Allendale, herself a subject of the brown-skinned king, though more of Anglo-Saxon blood ran in her veins than of Polynesian. In fact, the random breeds in her were so attenuated that they were valued at eighths and sixteenths. In the latter proportion was the blood of her great-grandmother, Paahao—the Princess Paahao, for she came of the royal line. Stella Allendale's great-grandfather had been a Captain Blunt, an English adventurer who took service under Kamehameha I. and was made a tabu chief himself. Her grandfather had been a New Bedford whaling captain, while though her own father had been introduced a remote blend of Italian and Portuguese which had been grafted upon his own English stock. Legally a Hawaiian, Ah Chun's spouse was more of any one of three other nationalities.

And into this conglomerate of the races, Ah Chun introduced the Mongolian mixture. Thus, his children by Mrs. Ah Chun were one thirty-second Polynesian, one-sixteenth Italian, one-sixteenth Portuguese, one-half Chinese, and eleven thirty-seconds English and American. It might well be that Ah Chun would have refrained from matrimony could he have foreseen the wonderful family that was to spring from this union. It was wonderful in many ways. First, there was its size. There were fifteen sons and daughters, mostly daughters. The sons had come first, three of them, and then had followed, in unswerving sequence, a round dozen of girls. The blend of the races was excellent. Not alone fruitful did it prove, for the progeny, without exception, was healthy and without blemish. But the most amazing thing about the family was its beauty. All the girls were beautiful—delicately, ethereally beautiful. Mama Ah Chun's rotund lines seemed to modify papa Ah Chun's lean angles, so that the daughters were willowy without being lathy, round-muscled without being chubby. In every feature of every face were haunting reminiscences of Asia, all manipulated over and disguised by old England, New England, and South of Europe. No observer, without information, would have guessed the heavy Chinese strain in their veins; nor could any observer, after being informed, fail to note immediately the Chinese traces.

As beauties, the Ah Chun girls were something new. Nothing like them had been seen before. They resembled nothing so much as they resembled one another, and yet each girl was sharply individual. There was no mistaking one for another. On the other hand, Maud, who was blue-eyed and yellow-haired, would remind one instantly of Henrietta, an olive brunette with large, languishing dark eyes and hair that was blue-black. The hint of resemblance that ran through them all, reconciling every differentiation, was Ah Chun's contribution. He had furnished the groundwork upon which had been traced the blended patterns of the races. He had furnished the slim-boned Chinese frame, upon which had been builded the delicacies and subtleties of Saxon, Latin, and Polynesian flesh.

Mrs. Ah Chun had ideas of her own to which Ah Chun gave credence, though never permitting them expression when they conflicted with his own philosophic calm She had been used all her life to living in European fashion. Very well, Ah Chun gave her a European mansion. Later, as his sons and daughters grew able to advise, he built the bungalow, a spacious, rambling affair, as unpretentious as it was magnificent. Also, as time went by, there arose a mountian house on Tantalus, to which the family could flee when the "sick wind" blew from the south. And at Waikiki he built a beach residence on an extensive site so well chosen that later on, when the United States government condemned it for fortification purposes, an immense sum accompanied the condemnation. In all his houses were billiard and smoking rooms and guest rooms galore, for Ah Chun's wonderful progeny was given to lavish entertainment. The furnishing was extravagantly simple. Kings' ransoms were expended without display—thanks to the educated tastes of the progeny.

Ah Chun had been liberal in the matter of education. "Never mind expense," he had argued in the old days with Parkinson when that slack mariner could see no reason for making the *Vega* sea-worthy; "You sail the schooner, I pay the bills." And so with his sons and daughters. It had been for them to get the education and never mind the expense. Harold, the eldest-born, had gone to Harvard and Oxford; Albert and Charles had gone through Yale in the same classes. And the daughters, from the oldest down, had undergone their preparation at Mills Seminary in California and passed on to Vassar,

Wellesley, or Bryn Mawr. Several, having so desired, had had the finishing touches put on in Europe. And from all the world Ah Chun's sons and daughters returned to him to suggest and advise in the garnishment of the chaste magnificence of his residences. Ah Chun himself preferred the voluptous glitter of Oriental display; but he was a philosopher, and he clearly saw that his children's tastes were correct according to Western standards.

Of course, his children were not known as the Ah Chun children. As he had evolved from a coolie laborer to a multimillionnaire, so had his name evolved. Mama Ah Chun had spelled it A'Chun, but her wiser offspring had elided the apostrophe and spelled it Achun. Ah Chun did not object. The spelling of his name interfered no whit with his comfort nor his philosophic calm. Besides, he was not proud. But when his children arose to the height of a starched shirt, a stiff collar, and a frock coat, they did interfere with his comfort and calm. Ah Chun would have none of it. He preferred the loose-flowing robes of China, and neither could they cajole nor bully him into making the change. The tried both courses, and in the latter one failed especially disastrously. They had not been to America for nothing. They had learned the virtues of the boycott as employed by organized labor, and he, their father, Chun Ah Chun, they boycotted in his own house, Mama Achun aiding and abetting. But Ah Chun himself, while unversed in Western culture, was thoroughly conversant with Western labor conditions. An extensive employer of labor himself, he knew how to cope with its tactics. Promptly he imposed a lockout on his rebellious progeny and erring spouse. He discharged his scores of servants, locked up his stables, closed his houses, and went to live in the Royal Hawaiian Hotel, in which enterprise he happened to be the heaviest stockholder. The family fluttered distractedly on visits about with friends, while Ah Chun calmly managed his many affairs, smoked his long pipe with the tiny silver bowl, and pondered the problem of his wonderful progeny.

This problem did not disturb his calm. He knew in his philosopher's soul that when it was ripe he would solve it. In the meantime he enforced the lesson that, complacent as he might be, he was nevertheless the absolute dictator of the

Achun destinies. The family held out for a week, then returned, along with Ah Chun and the many servants to occupy the bungalow once more. And thereafter no question was raised when Ah Chun elected to enter his brilliant drawing-room in blue silk robe, wadded slippers, and black silk skull-cap with red button peak, or when he chose to draw at his slender-stemmed silver-bowled pipe among the cigarette and cigar-smoking officers and civilians on the broad verandas or in the smoking room.

Ah Chun occupied a unique position in Honolulu. Though he did not appear in society, he was eligible anywhere. Except among the Chinese merchants of the city, he never went out; but he received, and he was always the centre of his household and the head of his table. Himself peasant-born Chinese, he presided over an atmosphere of culture and refinement second to none in all the islands. Nor were there any in all the islands too proud to cross his threshold and enjoy his hospitality. First of all, the Achun bungalow was of irreproachable tone. Next, Ah Chun was a power. And finally Ah Chun was a moral para-gon and an honest business man. Despite the fact that business morality was higher than on the mainland, Ah Chun outshone the business men of Honolulu in the scrupulous rigidity of his honesty. It was a saying that his word was as good as his bond. His signature was never needed to bind him. He never broke his word. Twenty years after Hotchkiss, of Hotchkiss, Morter-son Company, died, they found among mislaid papers a memo-randum a loan of thirty thousand dollars to Ah Chun. It had been incurred when Ah Chun was privy counsellor to Kameha-meha II. In the bustle and confusion of those hey-day money-making times, the affair had slipped Ah Chun's mind. There was no note, no legal claim against him, but he settled in full with the Hotchkiss' Estate, voluntarily paying a compound in-terest that dwarfed the principal. Likewise, when he verbally guaranteed the disastrous Kakiku Ditch Scheme, at a time when the least sanguine did not dream a guarantee necessary —"Signed his check for two hundred thousand without a quiv-er, gentlemen, without a quiver," was the report of the secre-tary of the defunct enterprise, who had been sent on the for-lorn hope of finding out Ah Chun's intentions. And on top of the many similar actions that were true of his word, there was

scarcely a man of repute in the islands that at one time or another had not experienced the helping financial hand of Ah
Chun.

So it was that Honolulu watched his wonderful family
grow up into a perplexing problem and secretly sympathized
with him, for it was beyond any of them to imagine what he
was going to do with it. But Ah Chun saw the problem more
clearly than they. No one knew as he knew the extent to which
he was an alien in his family. His own family did not guess it.
He saw that there was no place for him amongst this marvellous
seed of his loins, and he looked forward to his declining years
and knew that he would grow more and more alien. He did
not understand his children. Their conversation was of things
that did not interest him and about which he knew nothing.
The culture of the West had passed him by. He was Asiatic to
the last fibre, which meant that he was heathen. Their Christ-
ianity was to him so much nonsense. But all this he would have
ignored as extraneous and irrelevant, could he have but understood the young people themselves. When Maud, for instance
told him that the housekeeping bills for the month were thirty
thousand—that he understood, as he understood Albert's request for five thousand with which to buy the schooner yacht
Muriel and become a member of the Hawaiian Yacht Club. But
it was their remoter, subtler desires and moral processes
that obfuscated him. He was not slow in learning that the mind
of each son and daughter was a secret labyrinth which he could
never hope to tread. Always he came upon the wall that divides
East from West. Their souls were inaccessible to him, and by
the same token he knew that his soul was inaccessible to them.

Besides, as the years came upon him, he found himself
harking back more and more to his own kind. The reeking
smells of the Chinese quarter were spicy to him. He sniffed
them with satisfaction as he passed along the street, for in his
mind they carried him back to the narrow tortuous alleys of
Canton swarming with life and movement. He regretted that
he had cut off his queue to please Stella Allendale in the pre-
nuptial days, and he seriously considered the advisability of
shaving his crown and growing a new one. The dishes his highly
paid chef concocted for him failed to tickle his reminiscent
palate in the way that the weird messes did in the stuffy rest-

aurant down in the Chinese quarter. He enjoyed vastly more a half hour's smoke and chat with the two or three Chinese chums, than to preside at the lavish and elegant dinners for which his bungalow was famed, where the pick of the Americans and Europeans sat at the long table, men and women on equality, the women with jewels that blazed in the subdued light against white necks and arms, the men in evening dress, and all chattering and laughing over topics and witticisms that, while they were not exactly Greek to him, did not interest him nor entertain.

But it was not merely his alienness and his growing desire to return to his Chinese flesh-pots that constituted the problem. There was also his wealth. He had looked forward to a placid old age. He had worked hard. His reward should have been peace and repose. But he knew that with his immense fortune peace and repose could not possibly be his. Already there were signs and omens. He had seen similar troubles before. There was his old employer, Dantin, whose children had wrested from him, by due process of law, the management of his property, having the Court appoint guardians to administer it for him. Ah Chun knew, and knew thoroughly well, that had Dantin been a poor man, it would have been found that he could quite rationally manage his own affairs. And old Dantin had had only three children and half a million, while he, Chun Ah Chun, had fifteen children and no one but himself knew how many millions.

"Our daughters are beautiful women," he said to his wife, one evening. "There are many young men. The house is always full of young men. My cigar bills are very heavy. Why are there no marriages?"

Mama Achun shrugged her shoulders and waited.

"Women are women and men are men—it is strange there are no marriages. Perhaps the young men do not like our daughters."

"Ah, they like them well enough," Mama Achun answered; "but you see, they cannot forget that you are your daughters' father."

"Yet you forgot who my father was," Ah Chun said gravely. "All you asked was for me to cut off my queue."

"The young men are more particular than I was, I fancy."

"What is the greatest thing in the world?" Ah Chun demanded with abrupt irrelevance.

Mama Achun pondered for a moment, then replied: "God."

He nodded. "There are gods and gods. Some are paper, some are wood, some are bronze. I use a small one in the office for a paper-weight. In the Bishop Museum are many gods of coral-rock and lava-stone."

"But there is only one God," she announced decisively, stiffening her ample frame argumentatively.

Ah Chun noted the danger signal and sheered off.

"What is greater than God, then?" he asked. "I will tell you. It is money. In my time I have had dealings with Jews and Christians, Mohammedans and Buddhists, and with little black men from the Solomons and New Guinea who carried their god about them, wrapped in oiled paper. They possessed various gods, these men, but they all worshipped money. There is that Captain Higginson. He seems to like Henrietta."

"He will never marry her," retorted Mama Achun. "He will be an admiral before he dies—"

"A rear admiral," Ah Chun interpolated. "Yes, I know. That is the way they retire."

"His family in the United States is a high one. They would not like it if he married... if he did not marry an American girl."

Ah Chun knocked the ashes out of his pipe and thoughtfully refilled the silver bowl with a tiny pleget of tobacco. He lighted it and smoked it out before he spoke.

"Henrietta is the oldest girl. The day she marries I will give her three hundred thousand dollars. That will fetch that Captain Higginson and his high family along with him. Let the word go out to him. I leave it to you."

And Ah Chun sat and smoked on, and in the curling smoke-wreaths he saw take shape the face and figure of Toy Shuey—Toy Shuey, the maid of all work in his uncle's house in the Cantonese village, whose work was never done and who received for a whole year's work one dollar. And he saw his youthful self arise in the curling smoke, his youthful self who had toiled eighteen years in his uncle's field for little more. And now he, Ah Chun, the peasant, dowered his daughter with three hundred thousand years of such toil. And she was but one daughter of a dozen. He was not elated at the thought. It struck him that it was a funny, whimsical world, and he chuckled aloud and startled Mama Achun from a revery which he knew lay deep in the hidden crypts of her being where he had never penetrated.

But Ah Chun's word went forth, as a whisper, and Captain Higginson forgot his rear-admiralship and his high family and took to wife three hundred thousand dollars and a refined and cultured girl who was one thirty-second Polynesian, one-sixteenth Italian, one-sixteenth Portuguese, eleven thirty-seconds English and Yankee, and one-half Chinese.

Ah Chun's munificence had its effect. His daughters became suddenly eligible and desirable. Clara was the next, but when the Secretary of the Territory formally proposed for her, Ah Chun informed him that he must await his turn, that Maud was the oldest and that she must be married first. It was shrewd policy. The whole family was made vitally interested in marrying off Maud, which it did in three months, to Ned Humphreys, the United States immigration commissioner. Both he and Maud complained, for the dowry was only two hundred thousand. Ah Chun explained that his initial generosity had been to break the ice, and that after that his daughters could not expect otherwise than to go more cheaply.

Clara followed Maud, and thereafter, for a space of two years, there was a continuous round of weddings in the bungalow. In the meantime Ah Chun had not been idle. Investment after investment was called in. He sold out his interests in a score of enterprises, and step by step, so as not to cause a slump in the market, he disposed of his large holdings in real estate. Toward the last he did precipitate a slump and sold at sacrifice. What caused this haste were the squalls he saw already rising above the horizon. By the time Lucille was married, echoes of bickerings and jealousies were already rumbling in his ears. The air was thick with schemes and counter schemes to gain his favor and to prejudice him against one or another or all but one of his sons-in-law. All of which was not conducive to the peace and repose he had planned for his old age.

He hastened his efforts. For a long time he had been in correspondence with the chief banks in Shanghai and Macao Every steamer for several years had carried away drafts drawn in favor of one, Chun Ah Chun. for deposit in those Far Eastern banks. The drafts now became heavier. His two youngest daughters were not yet married. He did not wait, but dowered them with a hundred thousand each, which sums lay in the Bank of Hawaii, drawing interest and awaiting their wedding day. Albert took over the business of the firm of Ah Chun & Ah Yung, Harold, the eldest, having elected to take a quarter of a million and go to England to live. Charles, the youngest, took a hundred thousand, a legal guardian, and a course in a Keeley institute. To Mama Achun was given the bungalow, the mountain House on Tantalus, and a new seaside residence in place of the one Ah Chun sold to the government. Also, to Mama Achun was given half a million in money well invested.

Ah Chun was now ready to crack the nut of the problem. One fine morning when the family was at breakfast—he had seen to it that all his sons-in-law and their wives were present —he announced that he was returning to his ancestral soil. In a neat little homily he explained that he had made ample provision for his family, and he laid down various maxims that he was sure, he said, would enable them to dwell together in peace and harmony. Also, he gave business advice to his sons-in-law, preached the virtues of temperate living and safe investments, and gave them the benefit of his encyclopedic knowledge of industrial and business conditions in Hawaii. Then he called for his carriage, and, in the company of the weeping Mama Achun, was driven down to the Pacific Mail steamer, leaving behind him a panic in the bungalow. Captain Higginson clamored wildly for an injunction. The daughters shed copious tears. One of their husbands, an ex-Federal judge, questioned Ah Chun's sanity, and hastened to the proper authorities to inquire into it. He returned with the information that Ah Chun had appeared before the commission the day before, demanded an examination, and passed with flying colors. There was nothing to be done, so they went down and said good-by to the little old man, who waved farewell from the promenade deck as the big steamer poked her nose seaward through the coral reef.

But the little old man was not bound for Canton. He knew his own country too well, and the squeeze of the Mandarins, to venture into it with the tidy bulk of wealth that remained to him. He went to Macao. Now Ah Chun had long exercised the power of a king and he was as imperious as a king. When he landed at Macao and went into the biggest European hotel

to register, the clerk closed the book on him. Chinese were
not permitted. Ah Chun called for the manager and was treat-
ed with contumely. He drove away, but in two hours he was
back again. He called the clerk and manager in, gave them a
month's salary, and discharged them. He had make himself
the owner of the hotel; and in the finest suite he settled down
during the many months the gorgeous palace in the suburbs
was building for him. In the meantime, with the inevitable
ability that was his, he increased the earnings of his big hotel
from three per cent to thirty.

The troubles Ah Chun had flown began early. There were
sons-in-law that made bad investments, others that played
ducks and drakes with the Achun dowries. Ah Chun being out
of it, they looked toward Mama Achun and her half million,
and, looking, engendered not the best of feeling toward one
another. Lawyers waxed fat in the striving to ascertain the
construction of trust deeds. Suits, cross-suits, and counter-suits
cluttered the Hawaiian courts. Nor did the police courts escape. There were angry encounters in which harsh words and
harsher blows were struck. There were such things as flower-
pots being thrown to add emphasis to winged words. And
suits for libel arose that dragged their way through the courts
and kept Honolulu agog with excitement over the revelations
of the witnesses.

In his palace, surrounded by all dear delights of the Orient,
Ah Chun smokes his placid pipe and listens to the turmoil
over seas. Each mail steamer, in faultless English, typewritten
on an American machine, a letter goes from Macao to Honolulu,
in which, by admirable texts and precepts, Ah Chun advises
his family to live in unity and harmony. As for himself, he is
out of it all and well content. He has won to peace and repose.
At times he chuckles and rubs his hands, and his slant little
black eyes twinkle merrily at the thought of the funny world.
For out of all his living and philosophizing this remains to him
—the conviction that it is a very funny world.

The Sheriff of Kona

"YOU CANNOT escape liking the climate," Cudworth said, in reply to my panegyric on the Kona coast. "I was a young fellow, just out of college, when I came here eighteen years age. I never went back, except, of course, to visit. And I warn you, if you have some spot dear to you on earth, not to linger here too long, else you will find this dearer."

We had finished dinner, which had been served on the big *lanai*, the one with a northerly exposure, though *exposure* is indeed a misnomer in so delectable a climate.

The candles had been put out, and a slim, white-clad Japanese slipped like a ghost through the silvery moonlight, presented us with cigars, and faded away into the darkness of the bungalow. I looked through a screen of banana and lehua trees, and down across the guava scrub to a quiet sea a thousand feet beneath. For a week, ever since I had landed from the tiny coasting-steamer, I had been stopping with Cudworth, and during that time no wind had ruffled that unvexed sea. True, there had been breezes, but they were the gentlest zephyrs that ever blew through summer isles. They were not winds; they were sighs—long, balmy sighs of a world at rest.

"A lotus land," I said.

"Where each day is like every day, and every day is a paradise of days," he answered. "Nothing ever happens. It is not too hot. It is not too cold. It is always just right. Have you noticed how the land and the sea breathe turn and turn about?"

Indeed I had noticed that delicious, rhythmic intermingled breathing. Each morning I had watched the sea-breeze begin at the shore and slowly extend seaward as it blew the mildest, softest whiff of ozone to the land. It played over the sea, just faintly darkening its surface, with here and there and everywhere long lanes of calm, shifting, changing, drifting, according to the capricious kisses of the breeze. And each evening I had watched the sea-breath die away to heavenly calm, and heard the land-breath softly make its way through the coffee trees and monkey-pods.

"It is a land of perpetual calm," I said. "Does it ever blow here?—ever really blow? You know what I mean"

Cudworth shook his head and pointed eastward.

"How can it blow, with a barrier like that to stop it?"

Far above towered the hugh bulks of Mauna Kea and Mauna Loa, seeming to blot out half the starry sky. Two miles and a half above our heads they reared their own heads, white with snow that the tropic sun had failed to melt.

"Thirty miles away, right now, I'll wager, it is blowing forty miles an hour."

I smiled incredulously.

Cudworth stepped to the *lanai* telephone. He called up, in succession, Waimea, Kohala, and Hamakua. Snatches of his conversation told me that the wind was blowing: "Rip-snorting and back-jumping, eh?... How long?... Only a week?... Hello, Abe, is that you?... Yes, yes... You *will* plant coffee on the Hamakua coast... Hang your wind-breaks! You should see *my* trees."

"Blowing a gale," he said to me, turning from hanging up the receiver. "I always have to joke Abe on his coffee. He has five hundred acres, and he's done marvels in wind-breaking, but how he keeps the roots in the ground is beyond me. Blow? It always blows on the Hamakua side. Kohala reports a schooner under double reefs beating up the channel between Hawaii and Maui, and making heavy weather of it."

"It is hard to realize," I said lamely. "Doesn't a little whiff of it ever eddy around somehow, and get down here?"

"Not a whiff. Our land-breeze is absolutely of no kin, for it begins this side of Mauna Kea and Mauna Loa. You see, the land radiates its heat quicker than the sea, and so, at night, the land breathes over the sea. In the day the land becomes warmer than the sea, and the sea breathes over the land.... Listen! Here comes the land-breath now, the mountain-wind."

I could hear it coming, rustling softly through the coffee trees, stirring the monkey-pods, and sighing through the sugar-cane. On the *lanai* the hush still reigned. Then it came, the first feel of the mountain-wind, faintly balmy, fragrant and spicy, and cool, deliciously cool, a silken coolness, a wine-like coolness—cool as only the mountain-wind of Kona can be cool.

"Do you wonder that I lost my heart to Kona eighteen years ago?" he demanded. "I could never leave it now. I think I should die. It would be terrible. There was another man who loved it, even as I. I think he loved it more, for he was born here on the Kona coast. He was a great man, my best friend, my more than brother. But he left it, and he did not die."

"Love?" I queried. "A woman?"

Cudworth shook his head.

"Nor will he ever come back, though his heart will be here until he dies."

He paused and gazed down upon the beachlights of Kailua. I smoked silently and waited.

"He was already in love... with his wife. Also, he had three children, and he loved them. They are in Honolulu now. The boy is going to college."

"Some rash act?" I questioned, after a time, impatiently.

He shook his head. "Neither guilty of anything criminal, nor charged with anything criminal. He was the sheriff of Kona."

"You choose to be paradoxical," I said.

"I suppose it does sound that way," he admitted, "and that is the perfect hell of it."

He looked at me searchingly for a moment, and then abruptly took up the tale.

"He was a leper. No, he was not born with it—no one is born with it; it came upon him. This man—what does it matter? Lyte Gregory was his name. Every *kamaina* knows the story. He was straight American stock, but he was built like the chief-

tains of old Hawaii. He stood six feet three. His stripped weight
was two hundred and twenty pounds, not an ounce of which
was not clean muscle or bone. He was the strongest man I have
ever seen. He was an athlete and a giant. He was a god. He was
my friend. And his heart and his soul were as big and as fine as
his body.

"I wonder what you would do if you saw your friend,
your brother, on the slippery lip of a precipice, slipping, slipping, and you were able to do nothing. That was just it. I could
do nothing. I saw it coming, and I could do nothing. My God,
man! what could I do? There it was, malignant and incontest-
able, the mark of the thing on his brow. No one else saw it.
It was because I loved him so, I do believe, that I alone saw it.
I could not credit the testimony of my senses. It was too incredibly horrible. Yet there it was, on his brow, on his ears. I
had seen it, the slight puff of the earlobes—oh, so imperceptibly
slight. I watched it for months. Then, next, hoping against
hope, the darkening of the skin above both eyebrows—oh, so
faint, just like the dimmest touch of sunburn. I should have
thought it sunburn but that there was a shine to it, such an
invisible shine, like a little high-light seen for a moment and
gone the next. I tried to believe it was sunburn, only I could
not. I knew better. No one noticed it but me. No one ever noticed it except Stephen Kaluna, and I did not know that till
afterward. But I saw it coming, the whole damnable, unnamable
awfulness of it; but I refused to think about the future. I was
afraid. I could not. And of nights I cried over it.

"He was my friend. We fished sharks on Niihau together.
We hunted wild cattle on Mauna Kea and Mauna Loa. We broke
horses and branded steers on the Carter Ranch. We hunted
goats through Haleakala. He taught me diving and surfing until
I was nearly as clever as he, and he was cleverer than the average Kanaka. I have seen him dive in fifteen fathoms, and he
could stay down two minutes. He was an amphibian and a
mountaineer. He could climb wherever a goat dared climb. He
was afraid of nothing. He was on the wrecked *Luga*, and he
swam thirty miles in thirty-six hours in a heavy sea. He could
fight his way out through breaking combers that would batter
you and me to a jelly. He was a great, glorious man-god. We
went through the Revolution together. We were both romantic

loyalists. He was shot twice and sentenced to death. But he was too great a man for the republicans to kill. He laughed at them. Later, they gave him honor and made him sheriff of Kona. He was a simple man, a boy that never grew up. His was no intricate brain pattern. He had no twists nor quirks in his mental processes. He went straight to the point, and his points were always simple.

"And he was sanguine. Never have I known so confident a man, nor a man so satisfied and happy. He did not ask anything from life. There was nothing left to be desired. For him life had no arrears. He had been paid in full, cash down, and in advance. What more could he possibly desire than that magnificent body, that iron constitution, that immunity from all ordinary ills, and that lowly wholesomeness of soul? Physically he was perfect. He had never been sick in his life. He did not know what a headache was. When I was so afflicted he used to look at me in wonder, and make me laugh with his clumsy attempts at sympathy. He did not understand such a thing as a headache. He could not understand. Sanguine? No wonder. How could he be otherwise with that tremendous vitality and incredible health?

"Just to show you what faith he had in his glorious star, and, also, what sanction he had for that faith. He was a youngster at the time—I had just met him—when he went into a poker game at Wailuku. There was a big German in it, Schultz his name was, and he played a brutal, domineering game. He had had a run of luck as well, and he was quite insufferable, when Lyte Gregory dropped in and took a hand. The very first hand it was Schultz's blind. Lyte came in, as well as the others, and Schultz raised them out—all except Lyte. He did not like the German's tone, and he raised him back. Schultz raised in turn, and in turn Lyte raised Schultz. So they went, back and forth. The stakes were big. And do you know what Lyte held? A pair of kings and three little clubs. It wasn't poker. Lyte wasn't playing poker. He was playing his optimism. He didn't know what Schultz held, but he raised and raised until he made Schultz squeal, and Schultz held three aces all the time. Think of it! A man with a pair of kings compelling three aces to see before the draw!

"Well, Schultz called for two cards. Another German was

dealing, Schultz's friend at that. Lyte knew then that he was up against three of a kind. Now what did he do? What would you have done? Drawn three cards and held up the kings, of course. Not Lyte, he was playing optimism. He threw the kings away, held up the three little clubs, and drew two cards. He never looked at them. He looked across at Schultz to bet, and Schultz did bet, big. Since he himself held three aces he knew he had Lyte, because he played Lyte for threes, and, necessarily, they would have to be smaller threes. Poor Schultz! He was perfectly correct under the premises. His mistake was that he thought Lyte was playing poker. They bet back and forth for five minutes, until Schultz's certainty began to ooze out. And all the time Lyte had never looked at his two cards, and Schultz knew it. I could see Schultz think, and revive, and splurge with his bets again. But the strain was too much for him.

" 'Hold on, Gregory,' he said at last. 'I've got you beaten from the start. I don't want any of your money. I've got—'

" 'Never mind what you've got,' Lyte interrupted. 'You don't know what I've got. I guess I'll take a look.'

"He looked, and raised the German a hundred dollars. Then they went at it again, back and forth and back and forth, until Schultz weakened and called, and laid down his three aces. Lyte faced his five cards. They were all black. He had drawn two more clubs. Do you know, he just about broke Schultz's nerve as a poker player. He never played in the same form again. He lacked confidence after that, and was a bit wobbly.

" 'But how could you do it?' I asked Lyte afterward. 'You knew he had you beaten when he drew two cards. Besides, you never looked at your own draw.'

" 'I didn't have to look,' was Lyte's answer. 'I knew they were two clubs all the time. They just had to be two clubs. Do you think I was going to let that big Dutchman beat me? It was impossible that he should beat me. It is not my way to be beaten. I just have to win. Why, I'd have been the most suprised man in this world if they hadn't been all clubs.'

"That was Lyte's way, and maybe it will help you to appreciate his colossal optimism. As he put it, he just had to succeed, to fare well, to prosper. And in that same incident, as in ten thousand others, he found his sanction. The thing was that he did succeed, did prosper. That was why he was afraid of nothing. Nothing could ever happen to him. He knew it, because nothing had ever happened to him. That time the *Luga* was lost and he swam thirty miles, he was in the water two whole nights and a day. And during all that terrible stretch of time he never lost hope once, never once doubted the outcome. He just knew he was going to make the land. He told me so himself, and I know it was the truth.

"Well, that is the kind of man Lyte Gregory was. He was of a different race from ordinary, ailing mortals. He was a lordly being, untouched by common ills and misfortunes. Whatever he wanted he got. He won his wife—one of the Caruthers, a little beauty—from a dozen rivals. And she settled down and made him the finest wife in the world. He wanted a boy. He got it. He wanted a girl and another boy. He got them. And they were just right, without spot or blemish, with chests like little barrels, and with all the inheritance of his own health and strength.

"And then it happened. The mark of the beast was laid upon him. I watched it for a year. It broke by heart. But he did not know it, nor did anybody else guess it except that cursed *hapa-haole*, Stephen Kaluna. He knew it, but I did not know that he did. And—yes—Doc Strowbridge knew it. He was the federal physician, and he had developed the leper eye. You see, part of his business was to examine suspects and order them to the receiving station at Honolulu. And Stephen Kaluna had developed the leper eye. The disease ran strong in his family, and four or five of his relatives were already on Molokai.

"The trouble arose over Stephen Kaluna's sister. When she became suspect, and before Doc Strowbridge could get hold of her, her brother spirited her away to some hiding place. Lyte was sheriff of Kona, and it was his business to find her.

"We were all over at Hilo that night, in Ned Austin's. Stephen Kaluna was there when we came in, by himself, in his cups, and quarrelsome. Lyte was laughing over some joke—that huge, happy laugh of a giant boy. Kaluna spat contemptuously on the floor. Lyte noticed, so did everybody; but he ignored the fellow. Kaluna was looking for trouble. He took it as a personal grudge that Lyte was trying to apprehend his sister.

In half a dozen ways he advertised his displeasure at Lyte's presence, but Lyte ignored him. I imagined Lyte was a bit sorry
for him, for the hardest duty of his office was the apprehension
of lepers. It is not a nice thing to go into a man's house and
tear away a father, mother, or child, who has done no wrong,
and to send such a one to perpetual banishment on Molokai.
Of course, it is necessary as a protection to society, and Lyte,
I do believe, would have been the first to apprehend his own
father did he become suspect.

"Finally, Kaluna blurted out: 'Look here, Gregory, you
think you're going to find Kalaniweo, but you're not.'

"Kalaniweo was his sister. Lyte glanced at him when his
name was called, but he made no answer. Kaluna was furious.
He was working himself up all the time.

" 'I'll tell you one thing,' he shouted. 'You'll be on Molokai yourself before ever you get Kalaniweo there. I'll tell you
what you are. You've no right to be in the company of honest
men. You've made a terrible fuss talking about your duty,
haven't you? You've sent many lepers to Molokai, and knowing
all the time you belonged there yourself.'

"I'd seen Lyte angry more than once, but never quite so
angry as at that moment. Leprosy with us, you know, is not a
thing to jest about. He made one leap across the floor, dragging
Kaluna out of his chair with a clutch on his neck. He shook
him back and forth savagely, till you could hear the half-caste's
teeth rattling.

" 'What do you mean? Lyte was demanding. 'Spit it out,
man, or I'll choke it out of you!'

"You know, in the West there is a certain phrase that a
man must smile while uttering. So with us of the islands, only
our phrase is related to leprosy. No matter what Kaluna was,
he was no coward. As soon as Lyte eased the grip on his throat
he answered:

" 'I'll tell you what I mean. You are a leper yourself.'

"Lyte suddenly flung the half-caste sidewise into a chair,
letting him down easily enough. Then Lyte broke out into
honest, hearty laughter. But he laughed alone, and when he
discovered it he looked around at our faces. I had reached his
side and was trying to get him to come away, but he took no
notice of me. He was gazing, fascinated, at Kaluna, who was

brushing at his own throat in a flurried, nervous way, as if to brush off the contamination of the fingers that had clutched him. The action was unreasoned, genuine.

"Lyte looked around at us, slowly passing from face to face.

" 'My God, fellows! My God!' he said.

"He did not speak it. It was more a hoarse whisper of fright and horror. It was fear that fluttered in his throat, and I don't think that ever in his life before he had known fear.

"Then his colossal optimism asserted itself, and he laughed again.

" 'A good joke—whoever put it up,' he said. 'The drinks are on me. I had a scare for a moment. But, fellows, don't do it again, to anybody. It's too serious. I tell you I died a thousand deaths in that moment. I thought of my wife and the kids, and ...'

"His voice broke, and the half-caste, still throat-brushing, drew his eyes. He was puzzled and worried.

" 'John,' he said, turning toward me

"His jovial, rotund voice rang in my ears. But I could not answer. I was swallowing hard at that moment, and besides, I knew my face didn't look just right.

" 'John,' he called again, taking a step nearer.

"He called timidly, and of all nightmares of horrors the most frightful was to hear timidity in Lyte Gregory's voice.

" 'John, John, what does it mean?' he went on, still more timidly. 'It's a joke, isn't it? John, here's my hand. If I were a leper would I offer you my hand? Am I a leper, John?'

"He held out his hand, and what in high heaven or hell did I care? He was my friend. I took his hand, though it cut me to the heart to see the way his face brightened.

" 'It was only a joke, Lyte,' I said. 'We fixed it up on you. But you're right. It's too serious. We won't do it again.'

"He did not laugh this time. He smiled, as a man awakened from a bad dream and still oppressed by the substance of the dream.

" 'All right, then,' he said. 'Don't do it again, and I'll stand for the drinks. But I may as well confess that you fellows had me going south for a moment. Look at the way I've been sweating.'

"He sighed and wiped the sweat from his forehead as he started to step toward the bar.

" 'It is no joke,' Kaluna said abruptly.

"I looked murder at him, and I felt murder, too. But I dared not speak or strike. That would have precipitated the catastrophe which I somehow had a mad hope of still averting.

" 'It is no joke,' Kaluna repeated. 'You are a leper, Lyte Gregory, and you've no right putting your hands on honest men's flesh—on the clean flesh of honest men.'

"Then Gregory flared up.

" 'The joke has gone far enough! Quit it! Quit it, I say, Kaluna, or I'll give you a beating!'

" 'You undergo a bacteriological examination,' Kaluna answered, 'and then you can beat me—to death, if you want to. Why, man, look at yourself there in the glass. You can see it. Anybody can see it. You're developing the lion face. See where the skin is darkened there over your eyes.'

"Lyte peered and peered, and I saw his hands trembling.

" 'I can see nothing,' he said finally, then turned on the *hapa-haole.* 'You have a black heart, Kaluna. And I am not ashamed to say you have given me a scare that no man has a right to give another. I take you at your word. I am going to settle this thing now. I am going straight to Doc Strowbridge. And when I come back, watch out.'

"He never looked at us, but started for the door.

" 'You wait here, John,' he said, waving me back from accompanying him.

"We stood around like a group of ghosts.

" 'It is the truth,' Kaluna said. 'you could see it for your-selves.'

"They looked at me, and I nodded. Harry Burnley lifted his glass to his lips, but lowered it untasted. He spilled half of it over the bar. His lips were trembling like a child that is about to cry. Ned Austin made a clatter in the ice-chest. He wasn't looking for anything. I don't think he knew what he was doing. Nobody spoke. Harry Burnley's lips were trembling harder than ever. Suddenly, with a most horrible, malignant expression he drove his fist into Kaluna's face. He followed it up. We made no attempt to separate them. We didn't care if he killed the half-caste. It was a terrible beating. We weren't interested.

I don't even remember when Burnley ceased and let the poor devil crawl away. We were all too dazed.

"Doc Strowbridge told me about it afterward. He was working late over a report when Lyte came into his office. Lyte had already recovered his optimism, and came swinging in, a trifle angry with Kaluna to be sure, but very certain of himself. 'What could I do?' Doc asked me. 'I knew he had it. I had seen it coming on for months. I couldn't answer him. I couldn't say yes. I don't mind telling you I broke down and cried. He pleaded for the bacteriological test. "Snip out a piece, Doc," he said, over and over. "Snip out a piece of skin and make the test."'

"The way Doc Strowbridge cried must have convinced Lyte. The *Claudine* was leaving next morning for Honolulu. We caught him when he was going aboard. You see, he was headed for Honolulu to give himself up to the Board of Health. We could do nothing with him. He had sent too many to Molokai to hang back himself. We argued for Japan. But he wouldn't hear of it. 'I've got to take my medicine, fellows,' was all he would say, and he said it over and over. He was obsessed with the idea.

"He wound up all his affairs from the Receiving Station at Honolulu, and went down to Molokai. He didn't get on well there. The resident physician wrote us that he was a shadow of his old self. You see he was grieving about his wife and the kids. He knew we were taking care of them, but it hurt him just the same. After six months or so I went down to Molokai. I sat on one side of a plate-glass window, and he on the other. We looked at each other through the glass, and talked through what might be called a speaking-tube. But it was hopeless. He had made up his mind to remain. Four mortal hours I argued. I was exhausted at the end. My steamer was whistling for me, too.

"But we couldn't stand for it. Three months later we chartered the schooner *Halcyon*. She was an opium smuggler, and she sailed like a witch. Her master was a squarehead who would do anything for money, and we made a charter to China worth his while. He sailed from San Francisco, and a few days later we took out Landhouse's sloop for a cruise. She was only a five-ton yacht, but we slammed her fifty miles to windward into the northeast trade. Seasick? I never suffered so in my life.

Out of sight of land we picked up the *Halcyon*, and Burnley and I went aboard.

"We ran down to Molokai, arriving about eleven at night. The schooner hove to and we landed through the surf in a whale-boat at Kalawao—the place, you know, where Father Damien died. That squarehead was game. With a couple of revolvers strapped on him he came right along. The three of us crossed the peninsula to Kalaupapa, something like two miles. Just imagine hunting in the dead of night for a man in a settlement of over a thousand lepers. You see, if the alarm was given, it was all off with us. It was strange ground, and pitch dark. The lepers' dogs came out and bayed at us, and we stumbled around till we got lost.

"The squarehead solved it. He led the way into the first detached house. We shut the door after us and struck a light. There were six lepers. We routed them up, and I talked in native. What I wanted was a *kokua*. A *kokua* is, literally, a helper, a native who is clean that lives in the settlement and is paid by the Board of Health to nurse the lepers, dress their sores, and such things. We stayed in the house to keep track of the inmates, while the squarehead led one of them off to find a *kokua*. He got him, and he brought him along at the point of his revolver. But the *kokua* was all right. While the squarehead guarded the house, Burnley and I were guided by the *kokua* to Lyte's house. He was all alone.

" 'I thought you fellows would come,' Lyte said. 'Don't touch me, John. How's Ned, and Charley, and all the crowd? Never mind, tell me afterward. I am ready to go now. I've had nine months of it. Where's the boat?'

"We started back for the other house to pick up the squarehead. But the alarm had got out. Lights were showing in the houses, and doors were slamming. We had agreed that there was to be no shooting unless absolutely necessary, and when we were halted we went at it with our fists and the butts of our revolvers. I found myself tangled up with a big man. I couldn't keep him off of me, though twice I smashed him fairly in the face with my fist. He grappled with me, and we went down, rolling and scrambling and struggling for grips. He was getting away with me, when some one came running up with a lantern. Then I saw his face. How shall I describe the horror of it! It was not a face—only wasted or wasting features—a living ravage, noseless, lipless, with one ear swollen and distorted, hanging down to the shoulder. I was frantic. In a clinch he hugged me close to him until that ear flapped in my face. Then I guess I went insane. It was too terrible. I began striking him with my revolver. How it happened I don't know, but just as I was getting clear he fastened upon me with his teeth. The whole side of my hand was in that lipless mouth. Then I struck him with the revolver butt squarely between the eyes, and his teeth relaxed."

Cudworth held his hand to me in the moonlight, and I could see the scars. It looked as if it had been mangled by a dog.

"Weren't you afraid?" I asked.

"I was. Seven years I waited. You know, it takes that long for the disease to incubate. Here in Kona I waited, and it did not come. But there was never a day of those seven years, and never a night, that I did not look out on ... on all this ..." His voice broke as he swept his eyes from the moon-bathed sea beneath to the snowy summits above. "I could not bear to think of losing it, of never again beholding Kona. Seven years! I stayed clean. But that is why I am single. I was engaged. I could not dare to marry while I was in doubt. She did not understand. She went away to the States, and married. I have never seen her since.

"Just at the moment I got free of the leper policeman there was a rush and clatter of hoofs like a cavalry charge. It was the squarehead. He had been afraid of a rumpus and he had improved his time by making those blessed lepers he was guarding saddle up four horses. We were ready for him. Lyte had accounted for three *kokuas*, and between us we untangled Burnley from a couple more. The whole settlement was in an uproar by that time, and as we dashed away somebody opened up on us with a Winchester. It must have been Jack McVeigh, the superintendent of Molokai.

"That was a ride! Leper horses, leper saddles, leper bridles, pitch-black darkness, whistling bullets, and a road none of the best. And the squarehead's horse was a mule, and he didn't know how to ride, either. But we made the whale-boat, and as we shoved off through the surf we could hear the horses coming down the hill from Kalaupapa.

"You're going to Shanghai. You look Lyte Gregory up.
He is employed in a German firm there. Take him out to dinner.
Open up wine. Give him everything of the best, but don't let
him pay for anything. Send the bill to me. His wife and the
kids are in Honolulu, and he needs the money for them. I
know. He sends most of his salary, and lives like an anchorite.
And tell him about Kona. There's where his heart is. Tell him
all you can about Kona."

Good - by, Jack

HAWAII IS a queer place. Everything socially is what I may call topsy-turvy. Not but what things are correct. They are almost too much so. But still things are sort of upside down. The most ultra-exclusive set there is the "Missionary Crowd." It comes with rather a shock to learn that in Hawaii the obscure, martyrdom-seeking missionary sits at the head of the table of the moneyed aristocracy. But it is true. The humble New Englanders who came out in the third decade of the nineteenth century, came for the lofty purpose of teaching the kanakas the true religion, the worship of the one only genuine and undeniable God. So well did they succeed in this, and also in civilizing the kanaka, that by the second or third generation he was practically extinct. This being the fruit of the seed of the Gospel, the fruit of the seed of the missionaries (the sons of the grandsons) was the possession of the islands themselves, of the land, the ports, the town-sites, and the sugar plantations. The missionary who came to give the Bread of Life remained to gobble up the whole heathen feast.

But that is not the Hawaiian queerness I started out to

tell. Only one cannot speak of things Hawaiian without men-
tioning the missionaries. There is a Jack Kersdale, the man I
wanted to tell about; he came of missionary stock. That is, on
his grandmother's side. His grandfather was old Isaac Kersdale, a Yankee trader, who got his start for a million in the old
days by selling cheap whiskey and square-face gin. There's another queer thing. The old missionaries and old traders were
mortal enemies. You see, their interests conflicted. But their
children made it up by intermarrying and dividing the islands
between them.

Life in Hawaii is a song. That's the way Stoddard put it
in his "Hawaii Nei:"

"Thy life is music—Fate the notes prolong!
Each isle a stanza, and the whole a song."

And he was right. Flesh is golden there. The native woman
are sun-ripe Junos, the native men bronzed Apollos. They sing,
and dance, and all are flower-bejewelled and flower-crowned.
And, outside the rigid "Missionary Crowd," the white men
yield to the climate and the sun, and no matter how busy they
may be, are prone to dance and sing and wear flowers behind
their ears and in their hair. Jack Kersdale was one of these fellows. He was one of the busiest men I ever met. He was a several-
times millionaire. He was a sugar-king, a coffee-planter, a rub-
ber pioneer, a cattle-rancher, and a promoter of three out of
every four new enterprises launched in the islands. He was a
society man, a club man, a yachtsman, a bachelor and withal
as handsome a man as was ever doted upon by mamas with
marriageable daughters. Incidentally, he had finished his education at Yale, and his head was crammed fuller with vital
statistics and scholarly information concerning Hawaii Nei
than any other islander I ever encountered. He turned off an
immense amount of work, and he sang and danced and put
flowers in his hair as immensely as any of the idlers.

He had grit, and fought two duels—both political—when
he was no more than a raw youth essaying his first adventures
in politics. In fact, he played a most creditable and courageous
part in the last revolution, when the native dynasty was over-
thrown; and he could not have been over sixteen at the time.
I am pointing out that he was no coward, in order that you may
appreciate what happens later on. I've seen him in the breaking

yard at the Haleakala Ranch, conquering a four-year-old brute that for two years had defied the pick of Von Tempsky's cowboys. And I must tell of one other thing. It was down in Kona, —or up, rather, for the Kona people scorn to live at less than a thousand feet elevation. We were all on the *lanai* of Doctor Goodhue's bungalow. I was talking with Dottie Fairchild when it happened. A big centipede—it was seven inches, for we measured it afterward—fell from the rafters overhead squarely into her coiffure. I confess, the hideousness of it paralyzed me. I couldn't move. My mind refused to work. There, within two feet of me, the ugly venomous devil was writhing in her hair. It threatened at any moment to fall down upon her exposed shoulders—we had just come out from dinner.

"What is it?" she asked, starting to raise her hand to her head.

"Don't!" I cried. "Don't!"

"But what is it?" she insisted growing frightened by the fright she read in my eyes and on my stammering lips.

My exclamation attracted Kersdale's attention. He glanced our way carelessly, but that glance took in everything. He came over to us, but without haste.

"Please don't move, Dottie," he said quietly.

He never hesitated, nor did he hurry and make a bungle of it.

"Allow me," he said.

And with one hand he caught her scarf and drew it tightly around her shoulders so that the centipede could not fall inside her bodice. With the other hand—the right—he reached into her hair, caught the repulsive abomination as near as he was able by the nape of the neck, and held it tightly between thumb and forefinger as he withdrew it from her hair. It was as horrible and heroic a sight as man could wish to see. It made my flesh crawl. The centipede, seven inches of squirming legs, writhed and twisted and dashed itself about his hand, the body turning around the fingers and the legs digging into the skin and scratching as the beast endeavored to free itself. It bit him twice—I saw it—though he assured the ladies that he was not harmed as he dropped it upon the walk and stamped it into the gravel. But I saw him in the surgery five minutes afterward, with Doctor Goodhue scarifying the wounds and injecting permanganate of potash. The next morning Kersdale's arm was as big as a barrel, and it was three weeks before the swelling went down.

All of which has nothing to do with my story, but which I could not avoid giving in order to show that Jack Kersdale was anything but a coward. It was the cleanest exhibition of grit I have ever seen. He never turned a hair. The smile never left his lips. And he dived with thumb and forefinger into Dottie Fairchild's hair as gayly as if it had been a box of salted almonds. Yet that was the man I was destined to see stricken with fear a thousand times more hideous even than the fear that was mine when I saw that writhing abomination in Dottie Fairchild's hair, dangling over her eyes and the trap of her bodice.

I was interested in leprosy, and upon that, as upon every other island subject, Kersdale had encyclopedic knowledge. In fact, leprosy was one of his hobbies. He was an ardent defender of the settlement at Molokai, where all the island lepers were segregated. There was much talk and feeling among the natives, fanned by the demagogues, concerning the cruelties of Molokai, where men and women, not alone banished from friends and family, were compelled to live in perpetual imprisonment until they died. There were no reprieves, no commutations of sentences. "Abandon hope" was written over the portal of Molokai.

"I tell you they are happy there," Kersdale insisted. "And they are infinitely better off than their friends and relatives outside who have nothing the matter with them. The horrors of Molokai are all poppycock. I can take you through any hospital or any slum in any of the great cities of the world and show you a thousand times worse horrors. The living death! The creatures that once were men! Bosh! You ought to see those living deaths racing horses on the Fourth of July. Some of them own boats. One has a gasoline launch. They have nothing to do but have a good time. Food, shelter, clothes, medical attendance, everything, is theirs. They are the wards of the Territory. They have a much finer climate than Honolulu, and the scenery is magnificent. I shouldn't mind going down there myself for the rest of my days. It is a lovely spot."

So Kersdale on the joyous leper. He was not afraid of leprosy. He said so himself, and that there wasn't one chance in a million for him or any other white man to catch it, though

he confessed afterward that one of his school chums, Alfred
Starter, had contracted it, gone to Molokai, and there died.

"You know, in the old days," Kersdale explained, "there
was no certain test for leprosy. Anything unusual or abnormal
was sufficient to send a fellow to Molokai. The result was that
dozens were sent there who were no more lepers than you or
I. But they don't make that mistake now. The Board of Health
tests are infallible. The funny thing is that when the test was
discovered they immediately went down to Molokai and ap-
plied it, and they found a number who were not lepers. These
were immediately deported. Happy to get away? They wailed
harder at leaving the settlement than when they left Honolulu
to go to it. Some refused to leave, and really had to be forced
out. One of them even married a leper woman in the last stages
and then wrote pathetic letters to the Board of Health, pro-
testing against his expulsion on the ground that no one was so
well able as he to take care of his poor old wife."

"What is this infallible test?" I demanded.

"The bacteriological test. There is no getting away from
it. Doctor Hervey—he's our expert, you know—was the first
man to apply it here. He is a wizard. He knows more about leprosy than any living man, and if a cure is ever discovered, he'll
be that discoverer. As for the test, it is very simple. They have
succeeded in isolating the bacillus leprae and studying it. They
know it now when they see it. All they do is to snip a bit of
skin from the suspect and subject it to the bacteriological test.
A man without any visible symptoms may be full of the leprosy bacilli." .

"Then you or I, for all we know," I suggested, "may be
full of it now."

Kersdale shrugged his shoulders and laughed.

"Who can say? It takes seven years for it to incubate. If
you have any doubts go and see Doctor Hervey. He'll just snip
out a piece of your skin and let you know in a jiffy."

Later on he introduced me to Dr. Hervey, who loaded me
me down with Board of Health reports and pamphlets on the
subject, and took me out to Kalihi, the Honolulu receiving station, where suspects were examined and confirmed lepers were
held for deportation to Molokai. These deportations occurred
about once a month, when, the last good-bys said, the lepers

were marched on board the little steamer, the Noeau, and carried down to the settlement.

One afternoon, writing letters at the club, Jack Kersdale dropped in on me.

"Just the man I want to see," was his greeting. "I'll show you the saddest aspect of the whole situation—the lepers wailing as they depart for Molokai. The Noeau will be taking them on board in a few minutes. But let me warn you not to let your feelings be harrowed. Real as their grief is, they'd wail a whole sight harder a year hence if the Board of Health tried to take them away from Molokai. We've just time for a whiskey and soda. I've a carriage outside. It won't take us five minutes to get down to the wharf."

To the wharf we drove. Some forty sad wretches, amid their mats, blankets, and luggage of various sorts, were squatting on the stringer piece. The Noeau has just arrived and was making fast to a lighter that lay between her and the wharf. A Mr. McVeigh, the superintendent of the settlement, was overseeing the embarkation, and to him I was introduced, also to Dr. Georges, one of the Board of Health physicians whom I had already met at Kalihi. The lepers were a woe-begone lot. But here and there I noticed fairly good-looking persons, with no apparent signs of the fell disease upon them. One, I noticed, a little white girl, not more than twelve, with blue eyes and golden hair. One check, however, showed the sign. On my remarking upon the sadness of her alien situation among the brown-skinned afflicted ones, Doctor Georges replied:

"Oh, I don't know. It's a happy day in her life. She comes from Kauai. Her father is a brute. And now that she has developed the disease she is going to join her mother at the settlement. Her mother was sent down three years ago—a very bad case."

"You can't always tell from appearances," Mr. McVeigh explained. "That man there, that big chap, who looks the pink of condition, with nothing the matter with him, I happen to know, has a mark on his foot and another on his shoulder blade. Then there are others—there, see that girl's hand, the one who is smoking the cigarette. See her twisted fingers.

That's the anaesthetic form. It attacks the nerves. You could cut her fingers off with a dull knife, or rub them off on a nutmeg-grater, and she would not experience the slightest sensation."

"Yes, but that fine-looking woman there," I persisted; "surely, surely, there can't be anything the matter with her. She is too glorious and gorgeous altogether."

"A sad case," Mr. McVeigh answered over his shoulder, already turning away to walk down the wharf with Kersdale.

She was a beautiful woman, and she was pure Polynesian. From my meager knowledge of the race and its types I could not but conclude that she had descended from old chief-stock. She could not have been more than twenty-three or-four. Her lines and proportions were magnificent, and she was just beginning to show the amplitude of the women of her race.

"It was a blow to all of us," Dr. Georges volunteered. "She gave herself up voluntarily, too. No one suspected. But somehow she had contracted the disease. It broke us all up, I assure you. We've kept it out of the papers, though. Nobody but us and her family knows what has become of her. In fact, if you were to ask any man in Honolulu, he'd tell you it was his impression that she was somewhere in Europe. It was at her request that we've been so quiet about it.

"But who is she?" I asked. "Certainly, from the way you talk about her, she must be somebody."

"Did you ever hear of Lucy Mokunui?" he asked.

"Lucy Mokunui?" I repeated, haunted by some familiar association. I shook my head. "It seems to me I've heard the name, but I've forgotten it."

"Never heard of Lucy Mokunui! The Hawaiian nightingale! I beg your pardon. Of course you are a malahini (newcomer) and could not be expected to know. Well, Lucy Mokunui was the best beloved of Honolulu—of all Hawaii, for that matter."

"You say was," I interrupted.

"And I mean it. She is finished." He shrugged his shoulders pityingly. "A dozen *haoles*—I beg your pardon, white men—have lost their hearts to her at one time or another. And I'm not counting in the ruck. The dozen I refer to were *haoles* of position and prominence.

"She could have married the son of the Chief Justice if she'd wanted to. You think she's beautiful, eh? But you should hear her sing. Finest native woman singer in Hawaii Nei. Her throat is pure silver and melted sunshine. We adored her. She toured America first with the Royal Hawaiian Band. After that she made two more trips on her own account—concert work."

"Oh!" I cried. "I remember now. I heard her two years ago at the Boston Symphony. So that is she. I recognize her now."

I was oppressed by a heavy sadness. Life was a futile thing at best. A short two years and this magnificent creature, at the summit of her magnificent success, was one of the leper squad awaiting deportation to Molokai.

I recoiled from my own future. If this awful fate fell to Lucy Mokunui, what might not my lot be?—or anybody's lot? I was thoroughly aware that in life we are in the midst of death —but to be in the midst of a living death, to die and not be dead, to be one of that draft of creatures that once were men, aye, and women, like Lucy Mokunui, the epitome of all Polynesian charms, an artist as well, and well beloved of men—

I am afraid I must have betrayed my peturbation, for Doctor Georges hastened to assure me that they were very happy down in the settlement.

It was all too inconceivably monstrous. I could not bear to look at her. A short distance away, behind a stretched rope guarded by a policeman, were the lepers' relatives and friends. They were not allowed to come near. There were no last embraces, no kisses of farewell. They called back and forth to one another—last messages, last words of love, last reiterated instructions. And those behind the rope looked with terrible intensity. It was the last time they would behold the faces of their loved ones, for they were the living dead, being carted away in the funeral ship to the graveyard of Molokai.

Doctor Georges gave the command, and the unhappy wretches dragged themselves to their feet and under their burdens of luggage began to stagger across the lighter and aboard the steamer. It was the funeral procession. At once the wailing started from those behind the rope. It was blood-curdling; it was heart-rending. I never heard such woe, and I hope never to again. Kersdale and McVeigh were still at the other end of the wharf, talking earnestly; politics, of course, for both were head-over-heels in that particular game. When Lucy Mokunui pass-ed me, I stole a look at her. She was beautiful. She was beau-tiful by our standards, as well—one of those rare blossoms that occur but once in generations. And she, of all women, was doomed to Molokai. She walked like a queen, across the lighter, straight on board, and aft on the open deck where the lepers huddled by the rail, wailing, now, to their dear ones on shore.

The lines were cast off, and the Noeau began to move away from the wharf. The wailing increased. Such grief and despair! I was just resolving that never again would I be a witness to the sailing of the Noeau, when McVeigh and Kersdale returned. The latter's eyes were sparkling, and his lips could not quite hide the smile of delight that was his. Evidently the politics they had talked had been satisfactory. The rope had been flung aside, and the lamenting relatives now crowded the string-er piece in either side of us.

"That's her mother," Doctor Georges whispered, indi-cating an old woman next to me, who was rocking back and forth and gazing at the steamer rail out of tear-blinded eyes. I also noticed that Lucy Mokunui was wailing. She stopped abruptly and gazed at Kersdale. Then she stretched forth her arms in that adorable, sensuous way that Olga Nethersole has of embracing an audience. And with arms outspread, she cried:

"Good-by, Jack! Good-by!"

He heard the cry, and looked. Never was a man overtaken by more crushing fear. He reeled on the stringer piece, his face went white to the roots of his hair, and he seemed to shrink and wither away inside his clothes. He threw up his hands and groaned, "My God! My God!" Then he controlled himself by a great effort.

"Good-by, Lucy! Good-by!" he called.

And he stood there on the wharf, waving his hands to her till the Noeau was clear away and the faces lining her after-rail were vague and indistinct.

"I thought you knew," said McVeigh, who had been regarding him curiously. "You, of all men, should have known. I thought that was why you were here."

"I know now," Kersdale answered with immense gravity. "Where's the carriage?"

He walked rapidly—half-ran—to it. I had to half-run myself to keep up with him.

"Drive to Doctor Hervey's," he told the driver. "Drive as fast as you can."

He sank down in the seat, panting and gasping. The pallor on his face had increased. His lips were compressed and the sweat was standing out on his forehead and upper lip. He seemed in some horrible agony.

"For God's sake, Martin, make those horses go!" he broke out suddenly. "Lay the whip into them! Do you hear? Lay the whip into them!"

"They'll break, sir," the driver remonstrated.

"Let them break," Kersdale answered. "I'll pay your fine and square you with the police. Put it to them. That's right. Faster! Faster!"

"And I never knew, I never knew," he muttered, sinking back in the seat and with trembling hands wiping the sweat away.

The carriage was bouncing, swaying and lurching around corners at such a wild pace as to make conversation impossible. Besides, there was nothing to say. But I could hear him muttering over and over, "And I never knew. I never knew."